FAMILY PRACTICE

Community Nurse Gail Ingram always seemed to be accident prone around Dr Martin Hannerford, just when she most wanted to impress. When his father's death necessitated his return to the family practice in Dorset, Gail was astonished when Martin asked her to be his Practice Nurse. Surely he wouldn't have asked her if he didn't care about her ... but events in Dorset seemed to give the lie to Gail's hopes.

FAMILY PRACTICE

Family Practice

by

Sarah Franklin

Dales Large Print Books
Long Preston, North Yorkshire,
BD23 4ND, England.

British Library Cataloguing in Publication Data.

Franklin, Sarah
    Family practice.

    A catalogue record of this book is
    available from the British Library

    ISBN   1-84262-398-2 pbk

First published in Great Britain in 1990
by Mills & Boon Limited

Copyright © Sarah Franklin 1990

Cover illustration © Heslop by arrangement with
Allied Artists

The moral right of the author has been asserted

Published in Large Print 2005 by arrangement with
Jeanne Whitmee, care of Dorian Literary Agency

Dales Large Print is an imprint of Library Magna Books Ltd.

Printed and bound in Great Britain by
T.J. (International) Ltd., Cornwall, PL28 8RW

CHAPTER ONE

'Is that more comfortable?' Gail renewed the dressing on old Mrs Gallaway's knee and looked up at her patient. 'It's healing very nicely now. You were lucky not to break anything, you know, falling like that.'

The old lady smiled. 'I know, lovie. I've learned my lesson. I shan't be climbing on chairs any more, even to replace light bulbs. I'd rather sit in the dark.'

'There's a warden for things like that, you know,' Gail reminded her. 'I'm sure Mrs Wainwright is only too willing to help you.'

'I know that, dear.' Mrs Gallaway put her foot to the ground and gently eased her weight on to it. 'But it was late and I didn't like to bother her. She deserves her rest more than anyone.' She smiled. 'Now – you'll have that cup of tea?' The faded blue eyes looked at her. 'Do say yes, lovie. After all, this will be the last time I see you, won't it?'

Gail hesitated. She still had Mr Green's varicose ulcer to attend to and Mrs Vester's eye drops. She would have liked to spend more time with all of them on her last day, but time was running out fast. But, taking a look at the old lady's hopeful expression, she resigned herself to running late. After all, what was another half-hour? 'Of course, that would be lovely,' she said cheerfully, and was rewarded by the old lady's smile as she hobbled away to put the kettle on. Gail packed away her equipment and took off her disposable apron and gloves. She was going to miss visiting all her patients, but the thought of her new job sent a quiver of excitement up her spine. In spite of the fact that it wasn't really the kind of job she would have applied for normally, she could hardly wait to begin.

At number twenty-seven, Mr Green was his usual gruff self, submitting to Gail's ministrations with his usual grudging gratitude. 'Let's hope the new nurse isn't as clumsy as you are,' he growled.

'Like a bloomin' great elephant, aren't you?' It was the running joke between them – Gail being so slim and small. Mr Green knew all too well that Gail's feather-like touch would be hard to better, but he would never dream of saying so. Nevertheless, he had his own quirky way of showing his gratitude. As Gail was leaving he thrust a small package into her hand.

''Ere – take this.'

She looked at the little parcel in surprise. 'What is it, Mr Green?'

'Nothin' much. You said you liked it,' he

muttered. 'P'raps it'll remind you of me.' The lips under their bushy white moustache twitched. 'Serves you damn well right if it does!'

Gail unwrapped the parcel and found inside the little green china pig that had stood on Mr Green's mantelpiece. A lump came into her throat. 'Oh, thank you,' she said, laughing. 'Very appropriate – a green pig. How could it fail to remind me of you?'

'That's what I thought.' He joined in her laughter, his rusty voice rumbling like a drain. Gail put her hand on his shoulder and kissed the bristly cheek. 'Take care of yourself, you old rogue,' she said huskily. 'And behave yourself when Nurse Brent calls round. I've warned her about you. Just watch your language.'

The old man pretended to look scandalised. 'Language? Pure as the driven snow, my language is!'

Mrs Vester's eye drops didn't take long. She had just had her cataracts removed and was enjoying a new lease of life. She was full of her outing to play Bingo the previous evening and enthusiastic about the pleasure she got from the large-print books brought round by the mobile library.

On her way out of Medworth Court – the old people's flats – Gail met Mrs Wainwright, the warden.

'I hoped I'd catch you today,' the pleasant

11

middle-aged woman said. 'Your last day, isn't it? They're all going to miss you, you know. You're the most popular nurse we've ever had.'

'I'm going to miss them too.' Gail climbed into her car, waving as she switched on the ignition.

She *was* going to miss going out to meet the public, especially the old folk. Would she regret taking the job as practice nurse down in Dorset? she wondered. Then she thought of the beautiful countryside – and working with Doctor Martin Hannerford – and knew that she wouldn't.

The little town of Lullford sounded so picturesque – straight out of a Thomas Hardy novel. A far cry from industrial Northbridge with its pedestrian shopping precincts and its towering glass and concrete buildings. Several times lately she had actually had to remind herself that it was all really happening; that she was really leaving Northbridge behind to work with Martin Hannerford. It seemed almost too good to be true.

Gail had worked on the team of community nurses at the Northbridge Health Centre for two years, ever since qualifying. She'd enjoyed her work, although she never stopped missing her native countryside. The town often made her feel stifled and claustrophobic and she knew she would never get used to the way people lived in blocks of flats, one on top of the other like bees in a hive. She'd been considering changing jobs a year ago, but when Martin had joined the practice her plans had gone out of the window. It had been love at first sight as far as she was concerned, though that was a secret she kept strictly to herself. As for Martin, he hadn't even seemed to notice her existence.

Tall and dashing, with thick brown hair and the kind of smile that – as one of the Health Centre receptionists had put it – could melt reinforced steel at forty paces, he was instantly popular with patients and staff alike. Unmarried, he seemed to enjoy his bachelorhood to the full. He was certainly never short of female company. So Gail had been surprised when three months ago he had chosen to invite *her* out to dinner.

It had been a total disaster. She'd developed a cold on the morning of their date and, reluctant to postpone it, she had coughed and sneezed her way through the meal, meeting all his attempts at conversation in sniffling monosyllables. By the time he'd delivered her to the door of her flat her voice had almost gone and she'd only been able to croak a husky, 'Good'ight and thag you for a lubbly evedig.' It was hardly surprising that he hadn't asked her again. She'd spent weeks kicking herself. Why hadn't she played it cool and made him wait until she was better? It would have made him all the keener, she told herself miserably.

Then came the occasion when, in the absence of the practice nurse, he'd called her into his surgery and asked her to take a blood sample for him. It was a routine job she'd done a million times, but she'd been so nervous that she'd squirted the syringe up his sleeve instead of into the phial and spent the next ten minutes unsuccessfully mopping him up and apologising. Then there was Christmas. They'd met at the Health Centre staff party. Finding herself in charge of the drinks, Gail had managed to pour half a bottle of lime cordial over Dr Hannerford's expensive-looking hand-made shoes. After that she kept a low profile. It seemed she was fated to incur Martin Hannerford's contempt on every possible occasion. She was convinced that he had her down as a complete moron.

Unfortunately, none of it had made the slightest difference to the way she felt about him. She had only to see his tall, lean frame unfolding itself from his dark blue Porsche in the car park and her heart would flip. She didn't understand it. Until now she had always despised girls who had hopeless crushes on men. To her it seemed a waste of time and emotion that could be channelled into one's career. But that wasn't all – to her utter despair, she had taken to blushing at the merest mention of his name. So that when Martin was around she had to resort to looking the other way or hiding her face in a cupboard.

The news that he was leaving came like a bolt from the blue. Gail had just come in to pick up her messages one morning when she heard the receptionists, Pat and Helen, talking over their coffee. Pat looked up as she came in.

'Isn't it sad about Dr Hannerford's father?'

'Sad? Why – what's happened?'

'Haven't you heard? He died yesterday,' Helen told her in the breathy tone she reserved for the relaying of the bad news.

'And Martin has to leave almost immediately to take over the family practice,' Pat added.

Gail's heart sank like a stone and she busied herself with the notes in her file, shattered at the depth of her own dismay. 'That's in Dorset somewhere, isn't it?' She tried for a cool yet compassionate tone – and failed miserably.

'Lullford,' Pat supplied. 'They say it's a lovely place. I wouldn't mind going with him.' She peered into the mirror and tweaked at one of her chestnut curls. 'I wonder if they need a receptionist down there. I could do with a change. Maybe I'll ask him.'

Gail left the two of them fantasising

together. Martin had dated all the girls at the Centre at one time or another, but none had become special to him, as far as she could tell. But, in any event, Gail was far too realistic to allow herself fantasies of the kind they were weaving. Her encounters with him had been nothing short of catastrophic. No, Dr Hannerford would surely consider that leaving *her* behind was one of the disguised blessings to come out of his sad misfortune! She should be glad he was leaving, too. His presence had been far too distracting for her own peace of mind. All the same, she couldn't deny that the fact that he hadn't even bothered to say goodbye to her hurt.

Martin left the following morning to attend his father's funeral and rumours ran riot at the Health Centre. The general consensus seemed to be that he wouldn't be back. However, in spite of the rumours, three days later he *was* back. Gail walked into the office at the Centre and stopped in her tracks, surprised to find herself face to face with him. He looked up and smiled at her and her heart – over which she seemed to have no control where Martin was concerned – did its customary double back somersault. There was a crash as she dropped her case on the floor. Sinking to her knees to gather up its scattered contents gave her the opportunity she needed to hide her scarlet face. But when she looked up she found her nose two inches away from his cheek as he crouched to help her. As their eyes met she managed to say, 'I – I was sorry to hear about your father.'

'Thank you, Gail.' He handed her the last of her belongings and she stuffed it into her case and snapped it shut.

He held out a hand to help her up. 'Just off out on your rounds?'

'Yes.' She cleared her throat, acutely aware of the firm hand still cupping her elbow. 'I suppose you'll be leaving us quite soon?'

'I've promised to stay on for a couple of weeks,' he told her. 'Just till they can get a satisfactory locum. I'd like to stay longer, but I'm badly needed at home.'

'Of course. You'll be missed here – by the patients, I mean.' She longed to ask more questions but she felt she had no right. Backing away, she said, 'Well … I'll be going.'

She was halfway out of the door when he said suddenly, 'Gail … it would be nice if you'd have dinner with me one evening before I leave.'

She turned towards him, taking a deep breath and willing her cheeks to remain pale. 'That would be very nice … er … when?'

He smiled again. 'Whenever you're free. Tomorrow if you like.'

'Tomorrow…' She toyed with the idea of

17

saying she had another date, of making him wait, but her courage failed her. 'Tomorrow will be fine,' she said.

Picking up her hesitation, he frowned. 'Are you sure? I wouldn't want you to put anything off just for me.'

Was he laughing at her? She felt her colour rise painfully. 'Oh, no! I mean tomorrow is ideal, really.'

'Fine. I'll pick you up at around eight.'

Gail escaped, pink-faced and hating herself. Where was all the cool sophistication she'd promised herself? Where was the casual smiling nod – the slightly raised eyebrow that would make him feel that *he* was the lucky one?

Meeting briefly in the corridor the following morning, he told her that he'd booked a table at the Water Gypsy, a floating restaurant converted from one of the old grain barges and moored on a part of the river that had been transformed from its former sludgy squalor into a leisure area. Lawns swept down to the newly unpolluted water where swans and ducks swam beneath the trailing willows. Gail was thrilled. She had been longing to try the place – everyone had been raving about it ever since it opened.

That evening she took a lot of trouble over her appearance, standing for ages before the full-length mirror in her bedroom, trying to give her reflection an unbiased appraisal. The black jersey dress suited her fair colouring, she decided. She'd even be able to blush without looking too much like a boiled lobster – and she fully expected to blush. She was resigned to it. She wore the Victorian pearl pendant that had belonged to her aunt and brushed her blonde hair out in a change from its usual French pleat. The resulting long straight bob made her look younger and more vulnerable, but she decided that couldn't be helped.

He was on time. From her window she saw him get out of the dark blue car and run lightly up the steps of the building. He wore a dark grey suit and looked – to Gail – quite devastatingly attractive.

By the light of little Victorian lamps they ate the delicious seafood the Water Gypsy was becoming famous for, and under the influence of the refreshing white wine that Martin chose she found herself unwinding and telling him all about herself.

'I really envy you, going back to the countryside,' she told him. 'I grew up in the Cotswolds and I miss it.'

'Does your family still live there?'

Gail shook her head. 'My parents divorced when I was five. My father remarried and went to work abroad. My mother and I went to live with an aunt. She took care of me while my mother went back to work.'

'So you've no brothers or sisters?'

'No. I've never had what you could call a family life. My mother's career soon took off again and she went to work in London, only coming home at weekends. Then she met a new man and stopped coming home at all. When she remarried, I stayed on with my aunt. It seemed best that way.'

'Did *you* think so?' Martin was looking searchingly at her.

Gail shrugged. 'I was only eight at the time. I don't remember being asked.' She paused. 'I do remember feeling hurt and abandoned, though.' She smiled wryly at him. 'Do you know, that's the first time I've ever told anyone that.'

He smiled. 'I'm glad – that you felt you could tell me, I mean.' Refilling her glass, he asked, 'Is your aunt still living?'

'No, she died last year. She was great-aunt to my mother and very old.'

'You must miss her.'

'I do. Hers was the only home I ever really knew. I haven't seen my mother for years.'

'Poor little Gail.' His hand covered hers, but she pulled it away, blushing hotly.

'Oh, I wasn't complaining! Aunt Jessie gave me a very nice childhood. And I'm grown up now. I've got everything I want.'

'*Have* you? In that case I'd say you're luckier than most.' Martin's eyes drew hers and held them. She saw that he wasn't

20

patronising her as she'd thought and she wished she hadn't spoken so sharply.

'I'm sorry, Martin,' she said softly. 'It's just that I hate people being sorry for me. When I was little I had to put up with a lot of well-meaning people drooling over me. It always annoyed me. There was no need. And anyway, I soon learned that very few of them were sincere.'

'You sound cynical, if you don't mind my saying so.'

'Not cynical – just realistic.'

For a moment his gaze held hers, then he said, 'Yes, I can understand that.' There was a pause, then he asked, 'As a matter of interest, do you really have everything you want?'

She laughed. 'I walked right into that, didn't I? It was just a figure of speech. Have *any* of us?'

'I ask because I've been watching you,' he said. 'I've often caught you looking pensive and a little unhappy. Do you like your job?'

'I *love* the job. It's just the location I can't get used to. I used to be able to escape occasionally when Aunt Jessie was alive, but now that she's gone there's nothing to take me back there.'

'I must admit that I'll be glad to get back to Dorset, though there's a lot I shall miss about Northbridge.'

'It's the pace,' she said. 'The rush – the

21

never having time to "stand and stare" – there never being anything worth standing and staring *at!*'

He laughed. 'Exactly!'

They finished their coffee and Martin paid the bill. Outside it was dark now and the coloured lights that decked the Water Gypsy were alight, casting their multi-coloured reflections in the water. The spring evening air was soft and mellow and as they walked down the gangway Gail took a deep breath – then wrinkled her nose.

'See what I mean? You can *still* smell the chemical works in spite of all the window-dressing! At home, now, the air would be heavy with the scent of honeysuckle and wallflowers.'

He took her arm. 'Let's walk a little. We can pretend we're in the country. At least there are trees.' He looked down at her. 'Perhaps you'd better wrap up. It isn't all that warm.' He took the brightly coloured Paisley shawl she was carrying and draped it round her shoulders. As he did so, his fingertips brushed her neck and she shivered.

'You're cold,' he said. 'Perhaps you'd rather go for a drive?'

'No. I'm fine. I'd like to walk.' She could hardly tell him that the merest touch of his hand sent shivers up her spine. She didn't even like admitting it to herself. It sounded like something out of a really sloppy magazine story. To take her mind off the arm thrown carelessly across her shoulders she said, 'Tell me about Lullford and your family.'

In the dim light she saw his features soften as he answered, 'Lullford is beautiful. It's just as it's been for hundreds of years. But there's worry among the residents at the moment that it won't stay that way for much longer.'

'Oh – why is that?'

'They're about to start drilling for oil just off the coast. It'll mean an increase in the population and a lot of disruption to the peaceful life we've all enjoyed for so long. Though the contractors have promised to be as unobtrusive as they can.'

'Do you live near the sea?'

'Yes. In a house on the cliffs,' he told her. 'There have been Hannerfords in Lullford for seven generations.'

'And have you all been doctors?'

'No, I'm only the third generation.'

'I take it you do have brothers and sisters.'

'One of each,' he told her. 'My sister, Celia, is twenty-three and engaged to be married. My brother Patrick is the baby. He's only twelve. My mother died when he was born.'

'Oh, I'm sorry.'

'My Aunt Lottie keeps house for us all. She has ever since Patrick was born. She's my father's sister.' He chuckled. 'She's a bit of a tartar, but soft as a marshmallow underneath.'

'Tell me about the practice,' Gail said.

'Well, Dad used to be senior partner, then there's Dr Shires, and more recently Dr Grant, who's a kind of relation, has joined us.'

'So, now you'll be senior partner?' Gail turned to look up at him and caught a curious expression on his face. Pride mixed with something else she couldn't interpret.

'That's the general idea.'

They got to the end of the lamplit section of riverbank and turned back. Gail was acutely aware that the evening was almost over and felt a sharp pang of regret. This evening they had learned so much about one another. If only their first date could have been as successful. She closed her mind firmly to what might have been. It was too late now to speculate. In a few days Martin would be gone and she would have to do her best to try and forget him.

As he stopped the car outside her flat he switched off the ignition and turned to her. 'I've really enjoyed this evening, Gail. Thank you for coming out with me.'

She looked at him, just able to make out his features in the light from a nearby street lamp. 'No, thank *you*. I've enjoyed it all so much. I only wish...' She trailed off, unable to express what she was feeling, grateful for the dim light inside the car that hid her blush.

He leaned towards her, cupping her chin with his hand and lifting her face. 'You know, this evening has been something of a revelation to me. I thought you had it in for me.'

'Good heavens!' Her green eyes were round with astonishment as she looked at him. 'Why?'

He chuckled. 'All those subtle little hints, like squirting a blood sample all over my best shirt – pouring sticky cordial over my new shoes – not to mention doing your level best to infect me with your flu germs! And you always seemed to be going out of your way to avoid me.'

For a moment she stared into his eyes, lost for words. Then when he began to laugh, she joined in, the tension leaving her as she leaned against him, helpless with mirth. If only he knew! And, now that they had reached this new understanding, if *only* he didn't have to leave.

Tipping up her chin, he kissed her gently on the lips. 'You know, Gail, you're making me begin to wish I wasn't leaving after all.'

Drawing her closer he kissed her again, more deeply this time, and Gail told herself firmly that she must take it as light-heartedly as it was meant; after all, he must have said much the same to every girl he'd taken out since he'd been here. But it wasn't easy, pressed close to him like this, with the tangy scent of his aftershave in her nostrils and his cheek warm against hers.

She slept very little that night. Tossing from side to side, she alternated between gladness that she'd have this one memory to cling to and regret that she'd gone out with him tonight at all. If she *had* to disrupt her life by falling in love, why on earth did it have to be with a man about to walk out of her life for ever?

She hardly saw him at all in the busy days that followed and as the time for his departure drew nearer her heart grew heavier. She was realising with increasing dismay how difficult it was going to be not seeing him each day. Getting over her infatuation with Martin Hannerford wasn't going to be easy.

On his last day there was a small, informal party for him in the staff-room at the Centre. They had all clubbed together to buy him a leaving present; a smart leather-bound Filofax and a pen and pencil set. Dr Mays, the senior partner, made what Gail irritably considered to be a rather fatuous little speech and opened a bottle of champagne, making a great show of pouring them all a glass. Gail listened to them all giggling at the popping cork and fizzing bubbles, wishing that she could be anywhere but there.

Standing near the door, she joined them all in drinking Martin's health, then escaped to the cloakroom.

Coming out ten minutes later, she came face to face with Martin as he was on his way to clear the last of his things from his desk. He stared at her in surprise.

'Gail! You look like death. Are you all right?'

To her utter dismay her eyes filled with tears. Grabbing her arm, he bundled her across the corridor and into his room. Closing the door he took a clean handkerchief from his pocket and silently handed it to her.

She dabbed at her eyes, shamed by the spectacle she was making. 'I'm ... sorry. I think I've got a cold coming, or something. Oh, damn! I've put mascara all over your hanky now. Can I wash it and send it on to you?'

'Don't be silly.' He took it from her and stuffed it into his pocket. 'What's really the matter, Gail?'

She saw the concern in his eyes and couldn't meet them. Surely he must guess? 'It's just that I hate to see people leaving – you know – goodbyes.'

'I hate them, too, but it's more than that, isn't it? You're really unhappy here, aren't you?'

'No!' The denial came out in a thin, unconvincing wail.

There was a pause, then he said suddenly, 'Look, how would you like to come and work in Lullford?'

Her eyes widened. 'How could I do that?'

'We've never had a practice nurse and we really do need one. I know it's not what you'd normally be looking for, but it would tide you over while you look around. I dare say with the population expanding down there the local authority will be taking on more CNs. What do you say?'

She felt as though all the breath had been dashed from her body. It was so unexpected. Who would have thought half an hour ago that she'd be expected to make a spur of the moment decision like this?

'We could even put you up temporarily at Hannerford House,' he went on. 'There's plenty of room, so you'd have no need to worry about accommodation to begin with.'

He looked so pleased with himself. And she wanted so badly to say yes. 'I'd have to work out my month's notice here,' she said, trying to quell the rising excitement inside her.

'Of course. That's understood.'

'What about your partners – and your family?' she asked. 'Shouldn't you ask them first?'

He grinned. 'I'm not the senior partner and head of the family for nothing! What do you say? Do you want time to think about it?'

She paused, unable to frame the question she really wanted to ask. Did *he* want her to go? Or was he making the offer merely because he felt sorry for her? Instead she took a deep breath and said gravely. 'No, I'd like to accept your offer, Martin. Thank you.'

'Right. That's settled then.' He took a card from his pocket and passed it to her. 'I'll be leaving in about half an hour, but I'll write and confirm your appointment formally. You can give me a ring at the number on the card to make final arrangements.' He smiled. 'See you soon then, Gail.'

Suddenly she was alone in the corridor again, asking herself dazedly what she had done. She had just accepted a job hundreds of miles away – and all for the sake of a man. It was the kind of irresponsible action she would have despised another girl for. She could hardly believe she'd done it. Yet the feeling of excitement making her heart beat faster refused to be denied.

CHAPTER TWO

'Good evening, I'm Gail Ingram – Nurse Gail Ingram. I think you're expecting me.'

The young woman who had answered Gail's ring at the bell was tall and slim, dressed in jeans and a cotton shirt. The family resemblance was unmistakable. Gail knew by the girl's glossy dark hair and brown eyes that she must be Celia, Martin's sister.

'Oh, yes, come in.'

'My luggage...' Gail looked over her shoulder.

Celia Hannerford peered out on to the drive at Gail's five-year-old Metro. 'Is that your car?'

Was there a touch of disdain in her tone or had Gail imagined it? 'Yes,' she said. 'I'll get my cases from the boot and then perhaps you can tell me where I should park it?'

Celia frowned. 'There is some spare garage space round at the back. But you won't be staying *that* long, surely?'

'Oh – Martin said...'

'Oh, *Martin!* He's *always* saying things!' The girl laughed. 'Then, more often than not, he goes off and completely forgets

30

them! All right, get your things and come in. I'd leave the car till later if I were you. It won't be in the way.'

Somewhat dismayed, Gail put the larger of her two cases back into the boot and followed the girl into the house. Inside the hall she had an impression of blue and white: silky white wallpaper and paintwork and a deep blue carpet on the floor and the wide sweeping staircase that curved up to the first floor. Bowls of fresh flowers on the hall table and the window-sill on the half-landing made the air fragrant.

'I'm Celia Hannerford, Martin's sister, by the way.' The girl turned to Gail, offering a cool white hand.

'Who was that at the door? *Oh!*' A door to the right had opened to admit an elderly woman with greying hair. She wore a well-cut grey skirt with a white blouse, and a blue cardigan was draped around her shoulders.

'This is Miss Ingram, Martin's new practice nurse. Miss Ingram – this is my Aunt Lottie.' Celia turned to her aunt. 'I'll leave her in your hands. James will be here in an hour and I want to have a bath and change.'

Gail watched as the girl took the shallow stairs two at a time. The elderly woman at her side cleared her throat. 'You'd better come with me. I'll show you your room.' It seemed to Gail that the woman's shrewd

31

blue eyes swept her from head to foot – assessing her and finding her distinctly wanting. She led the way up the stairs, her long back ramrod-straight and her head erect.

At the end of the landing Aunt Lottie opened a door and stood aside for Gail to pass. 'I've put you in here. It's the house-keeper's room, but as we don't have a living-in housekeeper any more I thought you might as well have it. After all, it's only a temporary measure, isn't it? I think you'll be quite comfortable here for a day or two.'

Gail put down her case with some relief. 'Thank you, Miss Hannerford.'

The woman bridled. 'It's *Mrs Blake*, actually.'

Gail blushed. 'Oh, I'm sorry Martin said you were his father's sister, so I naturally assumed...'

'It's all right – so do most people. But I'm a widow, not a spinster. You'll find soap and towels by the washbasin. There's a bath-room two doors along. Dinner is at seven. If you want anything else–'

'Is Martin around?' Gail interrupted.

'Martin?' The woman stared at her. 'Martin isn't living here at present. He's moved into the flat over the surgery. There was an attempted break-in last week.' She sniffed disapprovingly. 'They were after drugs of course. All these *awful* new people we've been inundated with – I always said no good would come of it. Under the circumstances my nephew thought it would be best to remain on the premises until better security measures could be installed.'

'I see.' Gail felt disappointment wash over her. Was she to have dinner alone with these people who clearly resented her presence?

'He'll be along to eat with us, though, as it's your first evening,' the woman added grudgingly. Again the pale blue eyes appraised her, Gail had the impression that the woman was about to ask her something, but she seemed to change her mind. Turning, she said, 'I'll leave you to unpack.' Then she walked abruptly out of the room, closing the door behind her.

Gail looked round the room. It was comfortable enough, but the Hannerford family had made it plain that they didn't expect her to intrude on their privacy for long. She unpacked enough things for one night. First thing tomorrow she'd better start looking for somewhere to live.

The room was at the back of the house and its window looked down on to a pretty tiered garden. Directly below was a paved terrace with stone steps leading down on to a lawn. The garden dipped away in a series of shelves, ending in a tangle of shrubbery and trees, over the tops of which Gail could see the sea and she guessed that the garden ended at the clifftop. Perhaps there was a path down to the beach? In more welcoming circumstances she would have been enchanted. As it was…

She chose a red dress to wear for dinner. Its vibrant garnet colour gave her the confidence she badly needed to face a meal with the Hannerford family. Shaking out the creases, she slipped it on to a hanger and went off to find the bathroom.

Half an hour later, bathed and dressed, Gail ventured down the stairs. No one seemed to be about, but through an open door she glimpsed what looked like a drawing-room. Finding no one inside, she looked around her. The room was elegantly furnished in muted pinks and blues, the comfortable chairs covered in pastel chintzes. There was an antique writing desk by the window, on top of which family photographs were displayed. She stepped closer to look at them. There was one of Martin, taken some years ago, one of Celia, laughing up into the eyes of a fair-haired young man, obviously her fiancé, and another of a chubby baby boy. It was the fourth that puzzled her. It was of a beautiful auburn-haired young woman, dressed in mortar board and gown, a rolled degree held proudly in her hands. Martin had mentioned a sister and brother, so who was she? A sound from the hall startled her. She had no wish to be thought spying, and, moving across to the open window, she stepped out on to the terrace, deciding to explore what she had seen from upstairs.

In the garden the air was warm, filled with the fragrance of flowers. Out here it felt almost like home and Gail felt a stab of nostalgia for the little stone Cotswold house that had until recently been home to her. She walked down through each of the prettily laid out levels to the shrubbery at the bottom where she found a gate. Opening it, she ventured through.

'Hello! Who are you?'

Gail turned to see a boy with freckles and tousled brown hair emerging from under a bush. He wore tattered jeans and a dirt-streaked T-shirt and he carried a box with holes punched in the lid. 'Oh, I know!' He grinned up at her. 'You must be that nurse person they've been going on and on about.'

'I suppose I am.' Going on and on? What had they been saying, she wondered? 'And you must be Patrick.'

The boy winced. 'Rick, if you don't mind. Patrick's awful.'

'OK – Rick. I'm Gail.' She offered her hand, which he shook gravely. 'What's the box for?'

'Slugs.'

Now it was Gail's turn to grimace. 'Ugh! Why slugs?'

''Cos I like them,' Rick told her simply.

35

'They're my favourites – really interesting, they are. I've found four different kinds this afternoon. Want to see?' He began to take the lid off the box, but she held out a restraining hand.

'I'm not that keen on insects, thank you.'

The boy gave her a pitying look. '*Insects?* Slugs are land molluscs. *Pulmonata.* I thought everyone knew that!'

Gail grinned. 'Really? Well, I'll take your word for it.' She glanced down at his dishevelled state. 'Look, insects or not, I suppose you know it's almost dinnertime.'

Rick's mouth dropped open in dismay. 'Crumbs! It's not, is it? Aunt Lottie'll have my guts for garters!' He began to head for the house, then hesitated, turning back. 'Oh – nearly forgot. Put this in the summer house for me, will you?' He thrust the box of slugs into her reluctant hands and tore off, leaping up the terrace steps at breakneck speed.

Gail looked around her. The summer house. Where *was* the summer house?

It turned out to be a miniature log cabin, situated round at the side of the house, in a shady spot under a tall cedar tree, she was just about to open the door when a familiar voice hailed her, 'Gail!'

She turned. 'Martin! Hello!'

He was walking across the lawn towards her. 'So you found us all right then? I take it you've met everyone – settled in?' He looked down at the box in her hands. 'What's that?'

Gail laughed. 'It's a box of slugs, actually – or should I call them land molluscs? Four different kinds, so I'm told. I've been asked to put them in the summer house.'

Martin's face broke into a grin. 'No need to ask if you've met my revolting young brother!'

The box safely deposited he took her arm and headed for the house. 'You're looking much better than the last time I saw you. It's good to have you here, Gail.'

She began to blush with pleasure, but his next words showed that his delight at seeing her was purely practical.

'We're absolutely worked off our feet at the surgery with Frances away on this obstetrics course.' He looked down at her. 'Look, I know it's an imposition, but do you think you could possibly start first thing tomorrow?'

Swallowing her disappointment, Gail nodded. What she needed more than anything else to establish her in her new environment was work, she told herself.

Celia's fiancé, James, joined the family for dinner. He was a well-built young man with blond hair and seemed pleasant enough. But the conversation was distinctly stilted – polite but strained – and as they progressed

37

through the meal, from course to course, Gail grew more and more uneasy.

'What part of the country do you come from, Miss Ingram?' Mrs Blake enquired as the pudding was served.

'Oh, please, call me Gail. I used to live in the Cotswolds with my aunt, but she died last year.'

'I see.' The older woman regarded her coolly for a moment, then asked. 'Are your parents also dead?'

'No – they're divorced.'

Mrs Blake's eyebrows rose fractionally. 'Divorced? I see.' The words were heavily loaded with disapproval and the silence that fell over the table made Gail squirm.

'I shall have to try to find somewhere to live tomorrow,' she said, hoping that perhaps the family would feel more kindly disposed towards her if they knew she did not intend to impose on their hospitality for too long.

Martin looked up in surprise. 'Somewhere to live? You're going to find that practically impossible. There aren't even any digs to be found in Lullford now that the oil people have arrived. That was why I suggested you could put up here for a while. There's really no need for you to hurry, is there, Aunt Lottie? Especially now that Frances has moved out.'

The older woman shrugged. 'Why you

couldn't leave things as they were is beyond me,' she grumbled. 'We were all perfectly happy under one roof till–' She broke off, and applied herself to her food. 'Of course this is your house now, Martin. You must do as you like.'

'You're quite comfortable here, aren't you?' Martin looked at Gail enquiringly.

She nodded. 'Oh yes – very,' she said, avoiding the five pairs of eyes that seemed to have focused on her.

After dinner Martin announced that he was taking Gail down to look over the surgery. 'If she's to begin in the morning it'll save time,' he told them, pushing his chair away from the table.

In the car, Gail looked at him. 'Martin, your aunt doesn't seem happy about your living over the surgery. I wondered – couldn't *I* move in there?'

He shook his head. 'No, you'll be better off at the house. Until I've got a better alarm system, I think it's best that I stay there myself.'

'Only … it's just that…' Gail chewed her lip. 'I get the impression that your aunt doesn't take too kindly to the change. Maybe she thinks I'm responsible.'

'That's nonsense, of course she doesn't.' Martin looked at her. 'Has she been a bit cool with you?' Taking her silence for assent he went on, 'Take no notice of Aunt Lottie.

Her bark's worse than her bite.'

'I think I got off on the wrong foot by calling her Miss Hannerford,' Gail told him. 'I didn't know she was a widow.'

'Ah – that *is* a bit of a sore point with her. She married very young – in the last year of the war, her husband was killed only a few weeks later. Everyone has always assumed her to be unmarried and it irritates her.'

'I see. How sad.' Gail looked thoughtful. She'd discovered in the past that this kind of little quirk could often be traced back to a personal tragedy. To Mrs Blake it must seem as though her husband had never existed in the mind of others.

'I like your brother, Rick,' she said.

Martin chuckled. 'Well, at least you know where you are with him. You've only to admire his wildlife collection and he'll be your devoted slave for life!'

The surgery was at the end of Lullford's main street, close to the small market place. A large house had been converted into three surgeries, a reception office and a large waiting area. Martin showed her round all of these and then led her to another room next to the reception office. 'This used to be a store room,' he told her, opening the door. 'But we've had it cleared to make a nurse's room for you.'

It was a pleasant room, with a window

looking on to a paved yard at the rear. There was a desk and plenty of cupboard space, an examination couch and all the necessary equipment. Gail could still smell the fresh paint. They'd obviously gone to a lot of trouble.

'It's very nice – thank you.'

'No, thank *you* for joining us. And especially for agreeing to start right away. You *are* sure about that?'

Gail nodded. 'Work is what I came for. You said one of your partners was away on an obstetrics course, I think?'

'Yes, Frances – Dr Grant.'

'Has he been with you for long?'

Martin's eyebrows rose, then he laughed. '*She.* It's Fran*ces,* not Fran*cis.* And she's been with us for almost as long as I can remember, my parents adopted her when she was very young. We were brought up together.'

Suddenly Gail remembered the photograph of the lovely red-haired young woman on the writing desk and for some reason which she chose not to analyse, her heart plummeted. 'Ah – I see,' she said.

Martin watched her as she looked around the room. 'You seem uncertain. Is anything worrying you?'

'No. It's just – are you sure there's going to be enough work here for a practice nurse?'

'You'd better believe it!' He laughed. 'Why

else would I have offered you a job? Look, come into the office and I'll make some coffee and explain the situation.'

Over coffee he unfolded his plans for the future of the practice. 'We only have a small cottage hospital here in Lullford. Mothers have to go into Poole for ante-natal care and so on. Now that Frances is with us she's taking over all the gynae and obstetric work and we're hoping to have a Well Woman Clinic here, too – just basic screening to ease the load – so you see, there'll be plenty to keep you busy. There's something else, too – something I didn't know about before. The oil company has approached me and asked me to be their official physician.'

Gail looked up in surprise. 'Don't they employ one of their own?'

'They do, but they need one on the spot for emergencies. It's easier for them to employ a local GP. I may need you to help with that too.'

She smiled. 'I see what you mean.'

'Didn't I tell you so? We really couldn't manage without a practice nurse any longer. I could see that when I came home for Dad's funeral. Things had changed quite a lot since I left home. I could see you were unhappy at Northbridge – we got along well – you were the obvious choice.'

Gail nodded, swallowing a perverse sense of disappointment. What was the matter with her? She had wanted it to be a proper, official job, hadn't she? 'I'm sure it's going to be most interesting,' she agreed.

He studied her face for a long moment. She didn't look too sure. 'You're tired,' he said suddenly. 'I'm a thoughtless idiot, keeping you here when you've had a long journey already. Come on, I'll drive you home.'

'Oh, please – can't we walk?' Gail asked. 'I'd like to see a bit more of Lullford – get some fresh air before I go inside.'

They walked back to Hannerford House along the beach. The setting sun had turned the sea to a sheet of iridescent gold. It was silky calm, the wavelets lapping gently on the sand, but there was a chill in the air. Martin slipped an arm around her shoulders.

'Are you warm enough?'

'I'm fine.'

'It really is good to have you here, Gail.' His fingers tightened on her shoulder. 'I think we're going to work well together – the four of us.'

Gail soon saw that her earlier guess had been right. A path led from the beach up the cliffside to the garden of Hannerford House. They climbed it together. Martin took her hand, leading her up the twisting way that wound steeply through the thick wiry shrubs growing in wild profusion on the cliffside, warning her to watch out for the roots that broke the rough ground in places to trip the

43

unwary. By the time they reached the top she was breathless.

'I won't come in again,' Martin said. 'I've got some paperwork to catch up on. I hope you sleep well. Eight forty-five too early for you?'

'No.' Gail looked up at him in the failing light. 'I'll be there.'

'Sure you can find your way down to the surgery again?'

'Of course.'

'Well – goodnight, then.'

For a moment he paused, looking down at her, then he pulled her to him and kissed her briefly. 'Thanks again for taking the job, Gail. I'm really grateful.'

A moment later he was gone, quickly hidden from sight by the overgrown tangle of foliage. Gail stood there, his kiss still warm on her lips. She'd come to Lullford to fill a gap – to do a job, that was all. Well – wasn't that what she wanted? The new job would be different, but certainly interesting. But just how different would it be, working with Martin? Scarcely less difficult than living with his unwelcoming family, she told herself ruefully as she made her way back to the house.

CHAPTER THREE

Gail was at the surgery bright and early the following morning. She arranged the cupboards and drawers in her new room to her liking, familiarising herself with the whereabouts of all her supplies and equipment, so that she could lay her hands on the things she needed at a moment's notice. Finally, she added touches of her own to give the room a less clinical atmosphere. She made the acquaintance of Fay, the receptionist, and Madge, the middle-aged cleaning woman. Also, just before surgery, she met Dr Shires. He breezed into her room at five to nine and announced himself unceremoniously.

'Nurse Ingram, I presume?' He offered her his hand. 'I'm Peter Shires.'

Sandy-haired, he had the powerful, athletic build of a rugby player. His pink cheeks glowed with health and his bright hazel eyes reminded Gail of a robin's.

She put her hand into the strong broad one he held out to her and felt it gripped firmly. 'Hello, Dr Shires. I'm Gail.'

'Peter.' His smile was warm. 'I must say it's going to be great having our own nurse

45

– take a load off our surgery time, I can tell you. And Frances is going to be thrilled to bits with you.'

'When is she due back?' Gail asked.

'Day after tomorrow. We'll all be glad to see her – specially the patients. Martin and I have been seeing hers while she's been away and it hasn't been too popular with some of them.'

'Oh? Why is that?'

'It's our unhappy bachelor state.' He grinned. 'Most of the female patients like their doctors to be married – as married as possible – preferably with at least six offspring.'

Gail laughed. 'I see what you mean.'

'Yes…' He rubbed his chin. 'I keep telling myself I should do something about it, strictly for the patients' sake, you understand. But so far I haven't managed to con anyone into taking me on.'

Gail laughed again. 'Oh, hard luck. I'm sure you will before long, though.'

He winked at her saucily. 'Well – not for the want of working on it, I promise you.' He looked at his watch. 'Well, better go and start surgery I suppose.'

Gail soon found herself busy renewing dressings, removing stitches and taking blood for testing – all the routine jobs with which she was so familiar. More than once she thought of her patients at Northbridge

46

and wondered how they were liking Janet Brent. It seemed so odd remaining in one place all the time.

When surgery was over, Fay came through with coffee for her and a few moments later Martin put his head round the door.

'Sorry I didn't get time to look in before. I had an early call. Everything all right?'

'Fine, thanks.'

'I've brought you a list of the patients I shall be turning over to you – routine cases for injections and dressings – that kind of thing. I've asked Fay to look out all their cards so that you can familiarise yourself with their case histories.' He passed the list to her and perched on the edge of her desk as Gail glanced at it.

'You haven't installed a computer system yet, then, as we had at Northbridge?' she asked.

Martin grinned ruefully at her. 'We're out in the sticks down here, remember? No, much as I'd like it, I'm afraid economics won't run to it at the moment.'

Gail said nothing, but she couldn't help thinking of the affluent life-style at Hannerford House. There seemed to be no shortage of money there. But that was none of her business, she told herself.

'I see you've made yourself at home already.' Martin was looking round the room at the collection of soft toys ranged along a shelf; at the colourful mobile she'd hung from the ceiling above the examination couch and at the calendar on the wall behind the desk, with its glowing pictures of butterflies. 'You've added your own personal touches, I see.'

'I hope you don't mind. I find it relaxes the patients if the room looks more homely. And I like to provide something for the children to play with, to take their minds off whatever is happening.'

'Absolutely. Please feel free to do whatever you want. This is your domain to do as you like with. I hear you've met Peter.'

'Yes.'

He smiled. 'He couldn't wait to meet you. And now that he has he tells me that you're going to be a definite asset.'

'I hope he's right.'

'Gail…' Martin stood up and crossed the room to where she was standing, putting away the list he had given her in the filing cabinet. 'There's something I'd like to ask you. But I don't quite know how.'

As she turned, and found herself looking up into serious brown eyes, her heart skipped a beat. 'What – what is it, Martin?'

'Well – there's no surgery in the afternoons, as you know. Fay has two young children so, naturally, she can't come in until evening, when her husband is home. We have our car phones, of course, and we've been

48

using an answering machine for Reception, but it's far from ideal. I wondered – until we can get some extra part-time help, could you stand in on Reception, just for the afternoons?'

Gail didn't really know what she'd expected him to ask, but it certainly wasn't this. The let-down sharpened her tongue as she said crisply, 'It's not going to leave me much time for flat hunting, is it?'

He sighed. 'I really do hate asking you. Of course you must say no, if you feel you can't manage it.'

Biting her lip she turned away. 'No, of course I'll do it – as long as it really is temporary.'

'It is. I'm putting an ad in the local paper today.'

'All right, then. Do you want me to start today?'

'Could you? That would be marvellous.'

Gail turned away from his relieved face, reflecting that she might as well be here as at Hannerford House, where she felt in the way.

'So – do you think you're going to like it here?' Martin asked.

'I dare say I'll get used to it.' She began to tidy her desk, avoiding his eyes.

There was a pause, then he said, 'Right, I'll be on my way, then.' At the door he turned. 'You will talk to me if there's any problem, won't you, Gail?'

She did not look up. 'Yes, of course. Thank you.'

As the door closed behind him, Gail sank into her chair. How could she ever have imagined that any kind of close relationship could develop between them? He really *had* offered her this job simply because he needed a nurse. And what was even worse, he obviously saw her as a soft touch too – a dogsbody who would devotedly oblige in any way possible. She'd been a fool. A stupid, naïve fool.

'But you're stuck with it now, Gail Ingram, so you'd better make the best of it,' she told herself aloud. 'And the first thing to do is to get yourself out of that house and into somewhere of your own. Even if it's only a hovel!'

Manning the reception desk that afternoon, Gail had a chance to look through the local paper. Martin had been right, there wasn't a single flat advertised – not even a bedsit. There were houses for sale, of course, but it was clear that the oil company's arrival had pushed the prices up and after doing a few quick sums she saw that the mortgage repayments were going to be out of the question on her present salary. The thought of remaining indefinitely at Hannerford House, feeling like an unwelcome guest, made her feel depressingly trapped.

A few patients came in to pick up prescriptions or make appointments and the telephone rang fairly regularly, but apart from that there wasn't much to do. Then, just as she was thinking of putting the kettle on for tea, the outer door opened and a large young man walked in. He wore casual clothes and everything about him, from his broad shoulders to his strong, tanned face, spoke of the open air. Gail felt the power of his personality instantly.

'G'day, miss.' He grinned engagingly at her through the glass partition. 'Dr Martin Hannerford in?' His Australian accent was instantly recognisable.

'I'm sorry, no. He'll be in surgery this evening at six, though. Would you like to make an appointment?'

'Well, no. It's more of a business matter really.' His bright blue eyes were clearly admiring as he took in Gail's neat slim figure and blonde colouring.

'I'll see if I can raise him on his car phone for you, if you like,' she offered. 'If I could have your name?'

'Donaghue – Kev Donaghue,' he told her. 'Of Mellex Oil.'

'Oh!' As she dialled the number she remembered Martin mentioning that he was to be on call as emergency doctor for the oil company.

'Dr Hannerford.' Martin's voice came

51

through the car phone.

'I have a Mr Donaghue from Mellex Oil here in Reception for you,' Gail told him. 'Would it be possible for you to see him today?'

'I've finished my calls,' he told her. 'I was just about to come in for my messages anyway. If Mr Donaghue can wait...'

Gail glanced enquiringly at the man, mouthing, 'Can you wait?' He nodded.

'He'll wait for you here. Goodbye.' She glanced at the man. 'He's on his way. I'm sure he won't keep you waiting long. I was just about to make some tea. Would you like a cup?'

'Love it. Thanks.'

Gail opened the office door. 'Come through if you like.'

Kev Donaghue arranged himself in the chair she offered and regarded her with interest as she went about making the tea. 'You're new here, eh?'

'That's right. I started today.'

'Have you taken the place of the other lady?'

She looked at him. 'Oh, Fay, you mean? No. I'm the new practice nurse. I'm just filling in on Reception.'

'Nurse, eh? Local, are you?'

Gail blushed under his blatant admiration, beginning to wonder what business it was of his. 'No, though perhaps more local than

52

you are, Mr Donaghue,' she told him crisply.

He grinned, his blue eyes twinkling up at her. 'Fair enough! You could hardly be less local than me, I guess. So where do you hail from then?'

'Northbridge – in the Midlands.'

'Northbridge! That's interesting. Martin was telling me he used to work up there. Would it be a coincidence or did you know him before you came here?'

Annoyed, Gail gave him a straight look as she handed him his tea. 'I can't really see why it should matter to you where I worked before I came here, Mr Donaghue – or who I knew.'

The blue eyes opened innocently. 'No offence, miss – er, *Nurse*. I was just making polite conversation.' He looked up at her with mock contrition. 'Would it be an offence to ask your name?'

Gail felt herself colouring. She'd never encountered anyone quite like Kev Donaghue and she wasn't sure how to handle his particularly direct line of chat.

'I'm Nurse Ingram,' she told him stiffly.

He sipped his tea thoughtfully. 'Aw, c'mon! Nurse Ingram sounds like someone over sixty with a starched apron and moustache to match. I can't call you that. Didn't your mum and dad give you any other names?'

Her lips twitched in spite of herself. 'Gail,' she told him, relaxing a little.

'Gail, eh? That's better?' He took a long draught of his tea and looked up at her enquiringly. 'So, when's your day off, Gail?'

She stared at him. 'I only started work here today.'

'Well, if you're not doing anything after surgery this evening maybe we could have a drink or a bite to eat? I could show you the sights.'

'I don't think so.'

'Why not?'

'Because I have other plans.'

'What "other plans"?'

'Well – I'm looking for a flat, to begin with.'

'A flat? Pheew.' He whistled. 'I reckon you're gonna hit a king-size problem there.'

'So I've heard, but I have to try anyway.'

Kev Donaghue stood up and handed her his empty cup. 'Well, if you run into hitches, Gail, let me know. I just might be able to help you.' He stood looking down at her, his towering bulk seeming to dominate the small area behind the reception desk. 'Maybe when we know each other better you'll have that drink with me?'

'Give me one good reason why I should,' she challenged.

'Easy – you're my kind of girl.'

His audacity took her breath away. 'Really? How gratifying. I'll bear it in mind.'

Kev laughed, a big husky laugh that rang

through the building. 'That's what I mean! So cool and English. I bet you're a–'

Just what he was about to bet, Gail never found out. At that moment Martin walked in through the door. He looked from one to the other, then said stiffly, 'Perhaps you'd like to come through to the surgery, Mr Donaghue.'

As Gail opened the door to let him through, she caught the full force of the look he gave her. Obviously he had heard Kev's laughter and jumped to the wrong conclusion. And all of his accusations were clearly directed at her.

'Thank you for entertaining Mr Donaghue, Gail,' he said pointedly. 'Fay will be in shortly. You can go home now if you like.'

She watched as he disappeared through the doors. Kev, who was following, turned in the doorway to give her a conspiratorial wink before he too disappeared from view. She could have screamed with frustration. Martin had dismissed her as though she were a casual employee, not a colleague. Maybe that was how he saw her!

Arriving at Hannerford House, Gail found she had to ring the bell. She wondered what the reaction would be if she were to ask for a key, and decided it would not be looked on favourably. Rick opened the door.

'Oh, hello, it's you.' He was streaked with

dirt from head to toe and one knee was badly grazed and bleeding. His nose bore signs of a recent blow. Gail looked at him as she stepped into the hall.

'Whatever have you been doing to yourself?' she asked. 'Has your aunt seen you?'

'No. She's out. Everyone is.'

'Well, you'd better come up to the bathroom and let me clean you up before she comes back.' As they went upstairs together she asked him, 'What happened, Rick?'

'I fell,' he said non-committally.

'You haven't been fighting, I hope?'

As he went into the bathroom he glanced up at her. 'Well – only a bit.'

'What about?'

'Nothing much.'

'Who were you fighting with?'

'A friend of mine,' he told her, then looked up in surprise when she laughed. 'Well – he *used* to be a friend.'

'Well, come on, let's get that knee cleaned up, then I'll get some ice for your nose. That'll take the swelling down.'

Half an hour later they walked out into the garden together, Rick sporting a bandage on his injured knee. 'Do you think I'll have a black eye tomorrow?' he asked with interest.

'I don't think so. Just a fat nose.'

He nodded resignedly. 'And you won't tell Aunt Lottie? If she asks, you'll say I fell over?'

'I'll leave that to you.'

They walked down to the shrubbery in companionable silence and Rick showed his gratitude by revealing his secret place deep in the heart of the undergrowth. Here he had installed a couple of wooden boxes for seats. From inside one of them he retrieved a tin and began to take the lid off. Gail drew back apprehensively. 'Not more slugs?'

He grinned. 'No, liquorice allsorts. Have one?' He handed her the box. As she took one he regarded her thoughtfully. 'Are you really going to marry Martin?' he asked casually. She stared at him, the sweet halfway to her mouth as he added, 'Actually, I wouldn't mind having you for a sister-in-law.'

'Rick – what makes you ask a question like that?'

He shrugged. 'It's what they've been saying – when they think I'm not listening of course.'

'And they don't care for the idea, is that it?'

Rick shook his head. 'It's not 'cos of you. It's Frances, you see. They're all mad about Frances and they think Martin should marry *her!*'

'And what makes you think he's not going to?'

Rick shrugged. 'Dunno. You coming here – him wanting you staying in the house –

things like that, I s'pose. Aunt Lottie was cross – she said it wasn't fair on Frances when she was away and everything.' His question apparently forgotten, he stuffed his sweets back into their box and stood up. 'Come on, I want to show you an ants' nest I found yesterday.'

An hour later Gail was on her way into Lullford again for evening surgery. Now she had a much clearer picture. No wonder Celia and her aunt had greeted her so coolly. Martin and Frances had obviously been thought of as a couple in the family's eyes since childhood. But what of Martin? He must surely have been aware of the havoc he would cause – both to his family *and* to her, by bringing her here. Why couldn't he have made her position clear from the start? She was beginning to see him as totally insensitive. She sighed unhappily. It looked very much as though working here in Lullford wasn't going to work out at all.

To Gail's surprise, Martin appeared for dinner again that evening. He said he had to go through some papers of his father's and wanted to save time. The meal was a tense affair. Martin was still clearly annoyed with her about what he thought had happened in Reception that afternoon; Aunt Lottie was her usual taciturn self, but Celia was too full of her wedding plans to care about any of them. She chattered all through the meal about her dress, which she had chosen that afternoon, seeming oblivious of the atmosphere that hung over the table like a thunder cloud.

When the meal was over, Gail asked Martin if she could speak to him before he disappeared into his father's study. He agreed somewhat grudgingly and together they walked out into the garden, watched, Gail noticed, by a suspicious-looking Aunt Lottie.

'Mr Donaghue is a very friendly person,' she began. 'I hope you didn't think...'

As he turned to look at her she saw the same cold, hard look in Martin's eyes that she had seen this afternoon. 'There is a perfectly good waiting room. You didn't have to invite him in to tea!'

Taken aback, she paused. 'But, he wasn't a patient. I thought–'

'Donaghue is Mellex's chief engineer. He came to consult me about emergency arrangements. He's a good chap – up to a point, but he's a rough diamond. More used to male company. I wouldn't encourage him if I were you.'

Gail gasped. *'Encourage?* I didn't! Just what did you think we were doing?'

'It isn't hard to guess. I expect he was trying to make a date with you.'

'And what if he was?'

He smiled with maddening calm. 'You'd hardly allow yourself–'

'Are you a snob, Martin?' she interrupted. 'I wouldn't have thought so, but then I'm learning quite a lot about you, seeing you on your own home ground. If Kev Donaghue asks me to go out with him – and if I decide that I *want* to – I think that's my business, don't you?'

His brows came together in a frown. 'Naturally. You're perfectly free to do whatever you like. All I ask is that you keep your private affairs and your work at the surgery separate!'

'Thank you, I will!' Gail could hardly speak for the anger that throbbed in her chest. 'Oh, and while we're on the subject, perhaps you'll set the record straight with your family, Martin. They seem to be under the impression that there's some kind of relationship between us. And it doesn't seem too popular. Tell them it's all nonsense, will you?' And, turning, she walked away, taking with her the satisfaction of seeing his jaw drop in surprise.

'That's taken the wind out of your sails, Dr Hannerford,' she said, blinking back the angry tears that welled up in her eyes.

She retired to her room and stayed there for the rest of the evening, listening to her transistor radio. But, although there was a good play on, she found herself unable to concentrate. She was remembering the evening she'd spent with Martin at the Water Gypsy. Had he deliberately played on the fact that she was unhappy in North-bridge to lure her down to Dorset? Maybe he had even seen that she was hopelessly attracted to him and used the fact to the best advantage. The thought made her squirm with humiliation. She thought of the day he had left the Health Centre and the way she had let him see how upset she was. He must have seen it as an ideal opportunity to get an experienced nurse, familiar with up-to-date treatments, for his practice. How could she have been such a fool?

CHAPTER FOUR

Gail was getting ready for surgery the following morning when she heard sounds of excitement out in Reception. Fay and Madge's voices were raised and she could hear laughter and exclamations. She thought of opening the door to see what was going on, but decided against it. If it had anything to do with her, she would find out soon enough.

She had just changed into her uniform when there was a tap on the door, and on her answering call it opened to admit a young woman of about twenty-eight. Gail recognised the auburn hair and oval face immediately, but she also saw that the photograph at Hannerford House hadn't done Dr Frances Grant justice. She wasn't just pretty, she was beautiful with her vivid colouring and large expressive eyes. But her attractiveness went deeper than just her looks; it came from her outgoing personality, which gave her a kind of aura. She had the unconscious gift of making everyone she spoke to feel as though they were of special interest and Gail found herself warming to her at once, even before they had exchanged a greeting.

'Hello. I'm Frances Grant and you're Gail, our new practice nurse. I'm a bit late, I know, but welcome to Lullford.'

Gail took the hand the woman offered, returning her friendly smile. 'Thank you. It's nice to meet you, though of course I've heard all about you.'

Frances pulled a face. 'Ah, that sounds ominous. Good things, I hope?'

'Absolutely.'

Frances began to walk round, examining the room. She was a little taller than Gail; very slim with long shapely legs. She wore a simply cut green linen dress and white sandals.

'They've made a good job of the room, haven't they?' She turned to smile at Gail. 'I hope you like it. I can see that you've already added touches of your own. You've made it look very friendly.' She perched on one corner of Gail's desk. 'You know, I can't tell you how thrilled I was when Martin told me he'd been able to persuade you to take the job, Gail. He was quite excited that you'd agreed to come down to Dorset. We both feel we're very lucky to find you.'

'It promises to be a very interesting job. I'm sure you'd have had no trouble filling it,' Gail said.

Frances shook her head. 'You under-estimate yourself. The best we could have hoped for, down here in Lullford, would have been an older nurse, perhaps returning to work after bringing up a family. Which would have been fine, of course,' she added quickly. 'But you've been working in the community and you're obviously right up to the minute with everything.'

Gail remembered her thoughts of last night. Frances's words seemed to confirm them. The only things she disagreed with was that it was lucky. Martin had known exactly what he was doing when he had offered her the job. 'I hear you've been on an obstetrics course,' she said aloud. 'Did you find it interesting?'

Frances's bright blue eyes lit up. 'Oh, yes! I can't tell you *how* interesting, Gail. I expect Martin has told you that we're starting a Well Woman Clinic shortly. You and I will be working together on that as well as with our mother and baby patients. I hope it's the kind of work you enjoy.'

Gail enthusiastically admitted that it was. 'My work in the community was mainly with the older patients,' she said, 'obstetrics being the midwives' province. I missed it after leaving the hospital where I trained.'

'That's great. We must get together some time and have a good natter. I want our new clinic to be a success and I'd like to hear your ideas on how best to coax women at risk to come in for regular checks.'

'I'd like that.' Gail had expected to find it

difficult to like this paragon that Martin's family so badly wanted him to take for his wife. If she were truthful with herself, she hadn't really looked forward to meeting her. But, now that she had, she found it quite impossible not to respond to Frances's infectious warmth and enthusiasm.

Glancing at her watch, Frances got to her feet. 'Well, I'd better go and see if they've killed off all my patients.' But before she could reach the door it opened.

'Fran!' Martin held out his arms. 'Fay said she thought you were in here. It's great to have you back. You're looking *marvellous!*' He pulled her into his arms and hugged her warmly, lifting her clean off her feet. 'We've all been missing you like mad. Now that you're back we must lay on a practice meeting as soon as possible.'

Their excitement and pleasure at being reunited gave Gail a stab of jealousy. The feeling was alien to her and she was appalled at the sudden sharp pain it gave her. Since she had known Martin she had learned a lot about herself – some of which she would rather not have known. Resentful that her presence in the room seemed to have escaped Martin's notice, she cleared her throat.

Frances glanced around. 'I've just been making myself known to Gail as there was no one around to introduce me. We're going to get along fine, aren't we, Gail?'

'Yes, I'm sure we will.'

But Martin only gave her the briefest acknowledgement over Frances's shoulder before drawing her towards the door. 'Come and say a quick hello to Peter before we start,' he said, opening the door. 'I want to hear all about this course as soon–' The door closed behind them, shutting Gail off.

Gail had little time to ponder on the obvious warmth between Martin and Frances. From the moment surgery started that morning she found herself busy, the reason being that her list was slightly less routine than it had been so far. As she became used to the job, Martin and Peter were gradually passing over patients who no longer needed their care. To her surprise, one or two of the cases she dealt with were similar to those she had been used to in Northbridge. One of these was old Mr Oldfield with his ulcerated leg. No longer needing to be seen by Peter, he had been referred to Gail on arrival that morning, but he was far from happy with the new arrangements. He had enjoyed popping into the surgery once a week to chat to the doctor and have his leg dressed, and did not welcome the change.

Stumping into the surgery, he glared crossly at Gail. 'So you're this *practice nurse*, then? Well, I'll tell you straight, girl – I don't fancy no slip of a girl practising on *me!*'

Used to the elderly and their complaints, which usually stemmed from apprehension, Gail gave him her warmest smile. 'I'm not a nurse who is *practising*, Mr Oldfield,' she explained patiently. 'I'm the nurse who is working for this medical practice, and I can assure you that I'm fully qualified. Now, shall we have a look at your leg?'

Grudgingly, he submitted to having his trouser leg rolled up and his bandage removed. 'Thought I'd done with having young *women* fussing over me when I came out of hospital,' he muttered.

Ignoring his obvious prejudice, Gail chatted to him about her Northbridge patients – telling him about Mr Green who suffered from a similar complaint. 'He served in the war,' she told him. 'He was decorated, the Military Medal, I think he said.'

Mr Oldfield grunted. 'Huh! That's nothing. Ten a penny, they were. *I* got the George Cross!'

He launched enthusiastically into an account of how he won his medal in the Western Desert and it was with some difficulty that Gail finally managed to get him out of the surgery. Finally, she had to look at her watch and say regretfully, 'Oh, dear, look at the time. And just when I was enjoying our chat. Will you tell me the rest of it when you come in next week, Mr Oldfield?'

He nodded eagerly. 'I'll bring you my photograph album, if you like. I could pop back with it tomorrow.'

'No, next week will do. I'll look forward to it.' Gail ushered him out with a smile. It might have taken her a little longer than she'd intended, but at least she'd won him round.

Her last patient was a young man from the oil rig. He had suffered a badly cut hand in an accident at work and had come to have the stitches removed. Gail noticed that he looked pale as she opened the package containing the sterilised clippers and tweezers.

'You needn't worry. This won't hurt at all,' she said, putting on her surgical gloves. 'I'm sure it must have given you a lot of pain when it happened but it seems to be healing nicely now.'

The cut was between the thumb and fingers and clearly had been very deep, almost severing the thumb. There were stitches both on the back of the hand and on the palm. Very gently Gail snipped, carefully easing out each stitch, glancing at the young man as she did so. 'Can you bend your thumb easily?' she asked him.

He shook his head. 'I don't seem to have much use in it.'

Gently, she manipulated it and saw that it

was indeed weak and lacking in tone. 'I think it might be a good idea for you to have some physiotherapy at the hospital now that the stitches are out,' she told him. 'I'll ask the doctor to take a look at it.'

Martin had just seen out his last patient and came along to her room as soon as she called. Examining the man's hand, he agreed with Gail that a course of physiotherapy would help get the thumb working properly again and wrote out the necessary slip for him to take to the hospital.

When the patient had gone he looked at Gail. 'I hope you didn't find the extra patients too much.'

'No, not at all. I enjoyed the variety,' she said, realising for the first time that it was true. When she had arrived this morning she had felt that she had come to Lullford for all the wrong reasons, especially when she had seen the closeness that clearly existed between Martin and Frances. But work had made up for it. She would have to come to terms with her personal life in her own way, she told herself sensibly. And absorbing herself totally in her work was the best way to do it.

'You look very pensive, Gail,' he said. 'You're not still annoyed with me for what I said about Donaghue, are you?'

'Of course not.' Gail busied herself, tidying the room. 'I told you at the time how I

69

felt about that.'

He smiled. 'Yes, you certainly did, didn't you?'

Nettled by his obvious amusement, she went on, 'I'm sure you're right. We should all keep our personal affairs separate from work.'

He frowned and crossed the room to her. 'I get the impression that I'm supposed to glean something from that remark,' he said. 'But I'm afraid its significance escapes me.'

She turned to look at him. Now was the time to tell him exactly how she felt – to get things straight between them once and for all. 'Martin, I can see that you–'

A sudden scream startled her, stopping her in mid-sentence. From Reception came the sound of a child in obvious distress and the next moment the door burst open and Fay rushed in. When she saw Martin she looked surprised.

'Oh! I'm sorry, Doctor. I didn't know you were in here. There's a woman in Reception. Her little girl has just been involved in an accident. She's got a nasty head injury. I've told her she should go to the hospital but she refuses to go.'

Without a word Martin hurried out into Reception, Gail close behind him. A white-faced young woman stood in the reception hall, the screaming child in her arms. The front of her coat was stained with the blood that poured from a cut on the child's head and the little girl was screaming and thrashing about.

'Take the child,' Martin told Gail. 'We'll see to her in your room.' He took the young woman by the arm. 'Everything will be fine, don't worry. Just come along with Nurse and me.' Over his shoulder he said to Fay, 'I think a cup of tea would be in order if you can rustle one up.'

When they reached the nurse's room Gail was already cleaning the cut on the child's head, talking to her soothingly as she did so.

'What happened?' Martin asked the mother.

'She was in the back of the car,' the woman said. 'This cyclist suddenly came out of the side turning – just shot out right in front of me. How I didn't hit him, I'll never know! I stood on the brakes and – and Mandy shot forward. I'd fastened her in but she must have somehow released the belt catch. She hit her head on the dashboard.' The woman stifled a sob. 'I thought she was dead for a minute. She was so still and white, then she came round and began to scream.'

'Why didn't you drive straight to the hospital?' Martin asked. 'She really should have an X-ray as soon as possible to make sure there's no skull fracture.'

'She was rushed into hospital a few weeks ago with appendicitis,' the woman explained. 'It terrified her at the time. I didn't want her frightened again. She was scared enough when she saw all the blood.'

Martin nodded understandingly, examining the cut. 'Fortunately it isn't too bad,' he said. 'Children's head wounds always bleed alarmingly. But I strongly advise you to buy Mandy one of the car seats made specially for children.' He took the little girl from Gail and held her on his knee.

'Mandy, I'd like you and Mummy to go along to the hospital now to have a photograph taken. You know what a photograph is, don't you?' The little girl nodded solemnly, her big blue eyes concentrating on Martin's face. 'It won't hurt,' he told her, 'and Mummy will stay with you all the time. Will you be a good girl and do that for me?'

'Yes,' Mandy whispered.

Martin looked at Gail. 'We'll apply a steristrip, I think.' He continued to hold the child while she applied the special sterilised dressing that would hold the edges of the wound together. While she was doing it Fay came in with a cup of tea, which the woman accepted gratefully.

'I can't thank you enough, Doctor,' she said as she took Mandy from him.

'Not at all, that's what we're here for.' Martin smiled. 'Come back in a week's time and Nurse will take off the strip and make sure the cut is healing.'

As the door closed behind mother and child, Gail glanced at Martin. This morning she had seen a new, deeply caring facet of his character. His white shirt was liberally smeared with blood and he was going to run late for the rest of the day, yet he showed no signs of annoyance or frustration. He saw her looking at him and said, 'Don't worry. I always keep a spare shirt in my room. It won't take a minute to change.' In the doorway he paused. 'Gail, I'm sorry you didn't get to finish what you were going to say. Perhaps we could have dinner some evening soon?'

'Yes,' she said. 'I'd like that, Martin, perhaps we could.'

That afternoon Gail assisted Frances at their first ante-natal clinic together, and by the end of the afternoon she was forced to admit that she had thoroughly enjoyed herself. She found herself engrossed and fascinated. Clearly Frances was a dedicated and highly skilled doctor. By the time the afternoon's clinic was over and they were enjoying a cup of tea together Gail had quite forgotten her misgivings.

'I hear you're staying at Hannerford House,' Frances said, helping herself to a biscuit.

'For the moment. I hope to find myself a flat soon, though. Or even a bedsit.'

Frances's eyes twinkled at her over the rim of her cup. 'Aunt Lottie getting you down, eh?'

Gail found herself colouring. 'Oh, no! It's just that I like my independence. I'm used to being on my own.'

'She's quite an old sweetie in her own way – once you get to know her,' Frances said, ignoring Gail's denial. 'Rather one of the old school and a bit set in her ways, but very sincere for all that.'

Gail said nothing, preferring to reserve her judgement. Mrs Blake might be sincerely fond of members of her own family and Frances, but she had made it all too clear that she resented Gail's intrusion. Briefly, she wondered whether Martin had done as she had asked and put the older woman straight on the subject of their relationship.

'Is something wrong, Gail?'

'Wrong?' Gail coloured. 'No, of course not. I've enjoyed this afternoon enormously.'

'I meant up at the house. Celia's a lovely girl but she is a little preoccupied at the moment, as I don't doubt you've noticed. And young Rick can be a bit of a pest–'

'Oh, no! He's the only one who–' Gail broke off, biting her lip. 'We get along fine,' she said. 'He's a nice child.'

'That's good.' Frances took off her white

74

coat and began to put on her outdoor things. 'Sharing a home can be a little claustrophobic, even in a place the size of Hannerford House,' she remarked, taking out a compact and renewing her lipstick. 'Which is why I bought my cottage. You must come and see it some time.'

'A cottage? How lovely.'

Frances smiled. 'It used to be, but it's down by the harbour and the view isn't what it was, now that they're building an oil rig just off the point.' She snapped the compact shut and put it away. 'Still, they've promised that everything will return almost to normal once the rig is working, and we shouldn't stand in the way of progress, I suppose.'

'I met the company's chief engineer yesterday,' Gail told her.

'Kev?' Frances laughed. 'He's a great character. Did he try to date you?'

Gail blushed. 'Well...'

'If he did, you should go,' Frances advised. 'He's good company. You certainly wouldn't be bored.' She picked up her handbag. 'Well, I'm off; I must do some shopping. There isn't a thing to eat at my place at the moment.'

As Gail drove back to Hannerford House that evening the air was warm and humid. Summer had definitely arrived. Perhaps after dinner she'd go for a walk, after all, she'd hardly seen anything of Lullford yet. Frances had mentioned the harbour. Gail thought about the young woman doctor. Frances was too nice to resent, and, obviously, she couldn't know the devious method Martin had employed to get the fully experienced nurse they wanted for the practice. Anyway, it was her own fault for being so naïve and gullible, she told herself.

At dinner that evening the atmosphere seemed lighter. Maybe Martin *had* put his aunt's mind at rest, Gail reasoned. The talk was all of the arrival of summer.

'If it holds, could we have a barbecue on Sunday, Aunt Lottie?' Rick begged.

The older woman considered. 'Well ... it's early in the year yet, but we'll see.'

'The water's quite warm,' Celia said. 'I went in for a swim when I came in from work this afternoon.'

'I'll get my surfboard out,' Rick said excitedly. 'And Frances is home. She likes barbies. Maybe she'll come too.'

'Frances and Martin may have other plans,' Lottie Blake told him with a smug little smile at Gail. 'She's been away for some time, remember. They'll have a lot to talk over and this weekend will be their first chance to be together. They're bound to want a little time alone together,' she added, driving in the final nail.

Rick was looking at Gail. 'You'll come, won't you?'

'Well—'

'Oh, *do* come. It isn't any fun with only one or two. You and I can have swimming races.'

Gail hesitated, shy about admitting that she had never actually learned to swim.

'You mustn't make Nurse Ingram feel obliged to join us, Patrick,' Lottie Blake put in. She turned to Gail. 'But of course if you'd like to you'll be most welcome.'

Gail turned to look at her. She sounded quite sincere. Perhaps now that Frances was back she was no longer considered a threat to the Hannerford family – or was it that Martin had done a good job of reassuring his aunt? 'Thank you, I'd like to come,' she said. 'But you must let me help with the lunch, like everyone else.'

'Just as you wish.'

'Wow! *Great!*' Rick jumped up and down on his chair, but Gail looked at him wryly.

'I'll have to disappoint you about those races though, Rick. You see, I never learned to swim.'

When Gail came down to breakfast on Sunday morning there was a fine haze over the sea. An excited Rick informed her that it was a good sign. 'Look...' He pointed out of the dining-room window. 'If you can't see the end of Hemmingbury Point it's bound to be a hot day. When you *can* see it, it usually means it's going to rain.'

In the kitchen Gail found Celia and her aunt busy making salads and packing them into cool-boxes.

'Can I do anything?' she asked.

'There are two cooked chickens in the fridge,' Lottie Blake told her. 'You could cut them into pieces and pack them if you like.'

Gail noticed that the older woman looked less happy this morning and when she left the kitchen Gail asked Celia, 'Is your aunt all right? She isn't looking very well.'

Celia shrugged. 'It's Frances. Aunt Lottie rang her last night and she can't come to the barbie.'

'But she said herself that Frances and Martin would probably have something arranged,' Gail said.

'Ah, but Martin *is* coming,' Celia answered. 'Which means that they won't be spending the day together. *That's* what's bothering Aunt Lottie!'

'Your aunt is very fond of her, isn't she?' Gail ventured.

Celia looked up. 'She's always cherished a fond hope that they'd marry. I tell her that you can't manipulate people like that. If it happens, it happens.'

Gail worked on in silence. She wanted to

ask Celia what she thought. *Were* Martin and Frances close? They certainly seemed to be. But she couldn't help feeling a little stab of pleasure at the news that Martin was coming to the barbecue.

Rick had been right about the weather. The early morning mist had lifted by ten o'clock, revealing a smooth blue sea and a high azure sky, from which a blurred disc of sun promised real heat. Dressed in a pale blue cotton skirt and white T-shirt, Gail helped Celia carry the cool-boxes and baskets down to the beach, while Rick followed, carrying his surfboard.

By the time they had found a cool spot at the foot of the cliff to stow the lunch-boxes, Rick was already splashing in the water.

Celia threw herself full length on the sand. 'Look at him. He's like a little fish. A pity it's too calm for surfing, though.' She looked up at Gail. 'How come you never learned to swim?'

'When I was a child we lived inland.'

'Didn't you learn at school?'

'I never seemed to get the hang of it somehow,' Gail admitted. Both girls looked up as a cry from above heralded the arrival of James and Martin. James's arms were full of rugs and folding chairs, while Martin trundled the trolley with the folding barbecue. Aunt Lottie brought up the rear, carrying a bag containing flasks of coffee.

'I know it's warm but I thought we could all do with a cup,' she told them.

Gail watched as Celia and James went off to swim, envying their laughter and their smooth, competent strokes as they chased each other through the calm, clear water.

'Aren't you going in?' She turned as Martin sat down beside her on the sand.

She shook her head. 'I don't swim, I'm afraid.'

'Really? What a pity.' He studied her face for a moment. 'Am I forgiven?'

She flushed. 'For what?'

He smiled wryly. 'I think you know.'

'It isn't for me to forgive. You have a perfect right to object if my work isn't up to standard.'

'You know perfectly well that your work is more than satisfactory.'

'What happened was in working hours,' Gail insisted.

'Oh, come on. You thought I was an overbearing boor who ought to mind my own business. Admit it,' Martin challenged.

In spite of herself Gail laughed. 'Wel – you said it, not me.'

'So, will you accept my apology?'

'There's no need – really.' Gail glanced at him. He still wore jeans but had removed his shirt. She saw that his physique owed nothing to the cut of his suits. His shoulders and chest were broad and well-muscled, his flesh firm and golden. She looked away, annoyed to find herself colouring.

'Won't you at least sunbathe?' Martin asked, almost teasingly.

'I'm afraid I'm too fair. I burn dreadfully,' she told him.

'Celia has the same trouble but she has some marvellous cream,' he said. 'If you don't overdo it you should be all right.' He reached over to his sister's beach bag and found the tube, holding it out to Gail. 'Here, I'm sure she won't mind if you borrow a squeeze.'

'Thank you.' Slowly she removed her shirt to reveal the bikini top she wore underneath. Martin watched her, his eyes taking in her creamy, satin-smooth skin and gentle curves with undisguised appreciation. 'May I?' He was removing the top of the tube of sun cream and the next moment Gail felt his firm hand smoothing the cream into her back and shoulders.

After twenty minutes Martin advised Gail to put on her shirt again. 'I think I should go and swim with Rick,' he said, watching the boy. 'He hasn't said much, but he's really missing Father. Celia and I are all he has now. It's hard for children of elderly parents.'

Gail stood up and discarded her skirt. 'I'll come too. Maybe we can play with a ball or something.' For almost an hour the three of them played with Rick's beach ball, splashing in the shallows. Gail felt more relaxed than she had done since coming to Lullford. Watching Martin and his young brother she felt envious of their closeness. She had never known what it was to belong to a family.

They ate lunch – still deliciously cool from the insulated boxes – washed down with the bottles of wine that James had brought, with fresh fruit for dessert. As Martin stretched out on the sand afterwards, he said, 'That was wonderful. I think a cup of that coffee you brought would be appreciated now, Aunt Lottie.'

The older woman looked confused. 'Oh – I think there's a cup left.' She took one of the flasks from the bag and poured half a cupful, handing it to Martin.

He looked at it in surprise. 'Is this all there is? Who's been drinking it all?' He looked round at the others, but everyone looked blank. Gail began to gather up the used dishes and the picnic clutter, tidying it away. She had seen Aunt Lottie with a cup in her hand several times during the morning, but the older woman seemed too embarrassed to admit it, so she said nothing. Rick, however, was not so sensitive to his aunt's discomfort.

'Aunt Lottie drank all the coffee,' he said. 'I saw her.'

'Patrick! What a thing to say!' Aunt Lottie reddened.

'You did. You had *gallons* of it. I saw you swigging it!'

Lottie Blake's face went pink with fury. 'How dare you say such a thing?' she stormed. 'You're a very rude boy!'

'It doesn't matter. There's no need to get so upset,' Martin cut in. He put a hand on Rick's shoulder. 'Don't you know you should never accuse a lady of "swigging"?'

James laughed, breaking the tension. 'Tell you what, Rick. How would you like to come with Celia and me to watch cricket at the club?'

The boy was on his feet instantly. 'Wow! Yes, *please*, James.'

Aunt Lottie stood up. 'You must all do as you please. I'm feeling rather tired. I think I'll go and lie down.'

Martin looked at Gail. 'What are you doing?'

She shrugged. 'I hadn't planned anything.'

He raised an eyebrow. 'Would you like to go for a walk? There are parts of Lullford you haven't seen.'

'I'd like that.'

As she helped pack the picnic things up, she glanced at Lottie Blake and asked discreetly, 'Are you sure you're feeling all right, Mrs Blake?'

But the older woman bridled. 'I'm *quite* all

right, thank you,' she said. And Gail had the impression that her concern was misplaced. Martin helped carry the picnic things up to the house and Gail went to her room to change into a dress. She chose a crisp cotton one of coral and white with a full skirt and broad white sailor collar. As she changed into it she noticed that the sun had already dusted her nose with freckles and brought a soft golden glow to her skin. She pushed aside the thought that it could be the result of the promise of a whole afternoon alone with Martin.

They walked along the beach towards the more thickly populated part of the town. The warm sun had brought the tourists out and Martin showed her the cove for which the little town was famous and its rocky shore, honeycombed with caves that had once been a smugglers' paradise. It was crowded with families; children were playing among the rocks.

'Some time I'll show you the little church where they used to hide brandy and tobacco in the tower,' he promised. 'You can still see the rope marks where they hauled the kegs up. There are a dozen or so smugglers' graves in the churchyard too, complete with inscriptions.'

He took her hand and held it casually as they walked. Gail wondered if she was foolish to let such a small thing make her happy, knowing as she did that it meant less than nothing to him.

He glanced at her. 'You haven't regretted accepting the job here, Gail?'

'No.' She wished she could tell him that he needn't pretend any longer; that she wasn't a child, to be cajoled and cosseted. Instead she said, 'I like the work, and I like Frances very much.'

He smiled. 'I'm glad you get along, Gail – I have a special reason for wanting you to. You see–' A sudden cry made them both spin round. A boy who had been climbing the cliff and had ventured too far had fallen and lay still on the sand. His mother stood over him screaming hysterically. 'Help! Oh, God, *he's dead!* Help me, somebody!'

Instantly, Martin was running across the beach, followed by Gail. 'Stand aside, please. Let me see him. I'm a doctor.' Martin sank to his knees beside the motionless boy who Gail saw was about Rick's age. She turned, trying her best to calm the mother.

Martin lifted the boy's wrist to check the pulse and examined him carefully, lifting first one eyelid, then the other, to check the pupils. 'Did anyone see what happened?' he looked up to ask the onlookers. 'How far did he fall? Did he hit his head?' He turned to Gail. 'See if you can get someone to telephone for an ambulance.'

The boy's mother broke into fresh sobs at

the mention of an ambulance. 'Can you find me something to cover him with? He's in shock.' He grasped the woman's shoulders. 'Are you his mother?' The woman nodded and Martin went on, 'Please try to calm down. If he comes round and sees you like this he'll be frightened. Your son will be all right. As far as I can tell he's concussed and his collarbone is broken. I'd like to get him to hospital as soon as possible. If you're going to help him you *must* try to be calm.'

His quiet, firm voice seemed to have a soothing effect on the woman, who took a visible hold on herself. 'Thank you,' she whispered, biting her lip. 'There ... there's a beach towel and some sweaters in my bag. I'll get them.'

Gail went with her and they made the child as comfortable as possible.

The ambulance arrived and Martin carried the boy to it, negotiating the slippery cliff path as carefully as he could. As the child would be taken to the cottage hospital where there was no duty doctor, it was obvious that Martin would have to go with him. Their idyllic afternoon together had come to an abrupt end.

It was only later, alone in her room, that Gail remembered his half-finished sentence: 'I'm glad you and Frances get along, Gail. I have a special reason for wanting you to. You see–'

What could this reason have been – that Frances was soon to become Mrs Hannerford? Perhaps now she would never know. Perhaps she didn't want to.

CHAPTER FIVE

Gail attended her first practice meeting the following Monday evening after surgery and it was decided to hold the Well Woman Clinic on Wednesday afternoons, between two and four o'clock.

'I've arranged for notices to appear in the local paper and at the hospital,' Martin told them.

'I only hope we can persuade women to come along,' Frances said. 'It's so important and yet a lot of the clinics in larger towns have had to close through lack of support.'

'May I suggest something?' Gail put in.

All eyes turned in her direction. 'Of course, please do,' Frances said.

'I think we should stress that there is an informal atmosphere and that it isn't necessary to make an appointment. I'm sure more women would come if they could make up their minds on the spur of the moment. Making an appointment gives them time to imagine all kinds of horrors and dread going.'

'I agree. I think that's an excellent idea,' Peter said enthusiastically.

'And I wonder if there's a video we could

hire,' Gail went on. 'We could open one evening after surgery and show the video so that they could see what it's all about.'

'Great!' Frances was scribbling down some notes. 'I think I know where we can get one. I'll get on to it today. We'll put an ad in the paper for that, too. We could give them coffee and biscuits to make a relaxed atmosphere.' She smiled at Gail. 'Thanks for the suggestion, Gail.'

Later, as she was putting on her coat, Martin looked round the door. 'I thought you'd like to know that the boy I took to hospital yesterday afternoon was allowed home this evening.'

She smiled. 'Oh, that's good news.'

'He was lucky. Got away with concussion and a fractured collar bone. Young devil was halfway up the cliff before his mother realized he was gone. He won't do it again in a hurry, though.'

There was a pause. Gail wondered whether he was going to suggest taking her home. Instead he smiled and said, 'Thanks for your help, anyway, Gail. The mother asked me to pass on her thanks, too.'

'It was nothing. I didn't–' She stopped as Martin looked round at Frances who was passing on her way out.

'Oh, Fran, there's something I have to talk to you about. Come to the Plough for a drink.'

She looked up with a smile. 'All right. Are you ready now?'

The next moment they were both gone. Martin hadn't even looked back to say goodnight.

'Got time for a drink and a sandwich, Gail?' Peter stood in the reception area as she closed and locked her door.

For a moment she hesitated, about to refuse, then she asked herself, *why not?* She smiled at him. 'Yes! I'd like that very much.'

He laughed. 'That sounded almost defiant! Got it in for someone?'

They drove down to the Fisherman's Arms, a tiny pub on the harbour. Tables were set out along the harbour wall and they carried their drinks outside to enjoy the last of the evening sunshine. The sun rode low on the horizon and a cool breeze came off the sea, but it was pleasant after being inside all day.

'Is there anyone special back there in Northbridge, Gail?' Peter asked her.

She looked up at him in surprise. 'No, I'd hardly have come all this way if there were.'

'I just wondered. Sometimes I've caught you looking rather pensive,' he told her. 'You haven't found a flat yet, I suppose?'

'Haven't had time to look. There's nothing suitable advertised in the local paper.'

'Had you thought about buying?'

Gail gave him a rueful smile. 'I couldn't

90

afford the house prices down here on my salary.'

'I meant buying a flat.'

'Are there any for sale?'

Peter looked thoughtful. 'The oil people bought some houses and converted them, over on the other side of Lullford. The idea was that the men who worked on the rig would bring their families down here. Apparently it hasn't worked out quite as they'd expected, though. It seems that some of the flats are still going begging.'

'But would they sell one to a non-employee?'

Peter shrugged. 'That I can't tell you, but it's worth asking.'

'Thanks, Peter. Maybe I'll look into that.' She looked out to where the shape of the bulky rig could dimly be seen, far out to sea. 'Is the rig finished now?'

He nodded, taking a sip of his drink. 'Soon be fully operational, by all accounts.'

'Frances's cottage is somewhere down here, isn't it?' she asked him suddenly.

'It's over on the other side of the harbour. Drink up and I'll walk you over to see it.'

The cottage was one of a tiny terrace called Fisherman's Row. They were built of honey-coloured stone and had slate roofs. Each had a tiny front garden, bordered by a low wall. Peter told her that Frances lived in number four. The one with geranium-filled window boxes and a gleaming white front door.

'She's a great girl, Frances,' Peter said wistfully. 'The kind any guy would be lucky to get: a brilliant doctor, wonderful personality, very popular with the patients, a good cook and homemaker. And of course I don't have to tell you how devastatingly attractive she is.'

Gail glanced at him and saw with a small shock that he was in love with Frances. She sighed, feeling sorry for him. She knew all too well how he must feel.

They walked for a while, looking at the fishing boats bobbing at anchor on the water and at the houses that rose layer upon layer on the steeply sloping ground above the harbour. It was so peaceful and picturesque. But now the sun had finally dipped below the horizon out of sight. The sea had turned from golden to leaden grey and the refreshing breeze had developed a chilly bite. Gail shivered.

'Time to turn back, I think,' Peter said.

They retraced their steps in silence, each of them busy with their own thoughts, but, as they came in sight of Fisherman's Row again, they saw a car draw up outside number four. Two people got out. Even at this distance they were instantly recognisable. Peter looked at her, smiling wryly.

'Ah, I thought they might end up here. I

expect it's obvious to you, too, the way the land lies there.'

'Sorry?' Gail hedged, knowing all too well what he meant.

'Martin and Frances. I suppose it's inevitable. Everyone seems to take it for granted. And you have to admit that they make a stunning couple,' Peter said wistfully. 'If you ask me they're already secretly engaged – just waiting for a decent interval to pass after Martin's father's death before they announce it.'

'Do you really think so?'

He looked at her unhappy face and winced, raking a hand exasperatedly through his hair. 'Oh, God! What an idiot I am! I'm sorry, Gail. I should have realised.'

'Realised what?'

'We're in the same boat, aren't we – you and I? Now I know why you came all this way to take a job that was out of your province.' He dropped an arm across her shoulders. 'I'm sorry for rubbing it in, love. Believe me, I know how you feel. And don't worry, your secret's safe with me,' he added, anticipating her fears. The hand enclosing her shoulder tightened comfortingly. 'Look, come and have another drink. I think we both deserve one.'

They stayed in the Fisherman's Arms for an hour, listening to the local chatter and enjoying the atmosphere. Their mutual confessions seemed to have given them an affinity and to her surprise Gail found that she could relax with Peter.

'What was Martin's father like?' she asked him.

'A very fine doctor,' Peter said thoughtfully. 'But a difficult man to get to know. He kept himself very much to himself.'

'Were they a close family?'

Peter frowned. 'I wouldn't exactly say that. I think he expected rather a lot of Martin – sometimes for very little reward. He wasn't quick with the praise. He adored young Patrick, of course. And he seemed very fond of Frances.' He smiled wistfully. 'But, then, aren't we all?'

When they came out again it was almost dark. As they drove past Fisherman's Row, both carefully avoided drawing attention to the fact that Martin's dark blue Porsche was still parked outside number four.

Frances was successful in hiring a video about the Well Woman Clinic. Posters were put up in the surgery and in other prominent places in the town and on the night about twenty women arrived. Some were obviously just curious, but, as Frances said, it didn't matter as long as they went away and told their friends and sisters what they had seen. It was an all female evening. Fay and Madge came along to help with the

94

refreshments, while Frances and Gail stood by to answer any questions after the film had been shown.

The first question was about breast screening: a woman hesitantly asked what happened if a lump was detected. Frances got to her feet.

'As you saw in the video, the routine examination includes a breast check,' she told them. 'If a lump is found you would be referred for a mammography test at the hospital. This is the same as an X-ray. In all probability the fluid from the lump would be aspirated – drawn off with a hypodermic needle, which is relatively painless. And if the test on the fluid showed that it was a benign cyst – as I assure you ninety percent of lumps are – then there would be no more to be done.'

A murmur of surprised relief went round the room, then another voice asked, 'But if it *isn't – what then?*'

'This is always a possibility that has to be faced,' Frances told them frankly. 'If the lump is shown to be cancer, and a woman comes for treatment in the early stages, there is every hope of a complete cure. Which is why we feel that regular three-yearly checks at a Well Woman Clinic are so vitally important for women of all ages.'

'I couldn't face a mastectomy,' one woman remarked.

'I can assure you that surgeons realise nowadays how traumatic mastectomy is for a woman,' Frances told them. 'In many cases, nowadays, radical mastectomy can be avoided and, even if it *is* necessary, cosmetic surgery is now available, to avoid the mental anguish that women have been through in the past.'

'Does a smear test hurt?'

Frances smiled. 'Not in the least. And you will find only Nurse Ingram, here, and myself in attendance, so there's absolutely no need to feel embarrassed.'

Once the ice was broken the questions came in thick and fast, and even while they were having coffee many of the shyer women came up to either Frances or Gail with further queries. As they saw the last of the women out Frances smiled at Gail, sighing with relief. 'Well! I think we can safely say that was a success.'

Gail began to gather up the used cups. 'Next Wednesday afternoon will be the real test.'

Frances had some paperwork to do, so she left as soon as they'd tidied up, but Gail stayed on to help Madge and Fay wash up. As they were putting on their coats, Fay hung back a little. Madge went off to get her bicycle, calling out goodnight to them both, and Gail looked at Fay.

'Is your husband collecting you or would

you like a lift?'

'A lift would be great, but…' Fay chewed her lip thoughtfully.

'What is it, Fay? Did you want to ask me something?'

'Well – yes. Look – it might be nothing, but I've found this little lump.'

'How long ago did you find it?' Gail asked.

'It's been quite some time.' Fay looked unhappy. 'I went cold all over when Dr Grant said that about cancer needing to be treated early. It's Bob and the kids, you see. I don't know what they'd do without me. If I could just see them safely through school I'd be–'

'*Fay!*' Gail put her hands on the receptionist's shoulders. 'Stop it! Listen, I think you'd better let me have a look now. You've obviously been torturing yourself with this for weeks.'

In her room she examined Fay. Palpating the breast gently, she easily located the small lump Fay had described.

'Almost certainly a cyst,' she told her. 'But first thing in the morning we'll get Dr Grant to look at it, then we'll make you an appointment to see the consultant.' She smiled reassuringly. 'Get dressed now, Fay and stop worrying. The worst part is telling someone. Now that you've shared your worry you'll feel a lot better.'

Fay smiled shakily. 'Thank you, I do. I

haven't even told Bob.'

'Then I suggest you do so at once,' Gail admonished. 'That's what husbands are supposed to be for, isn't it?'

Gail dropped Fay off at her home and then went back to Hannerford House. When she arrived all the lights were out. She knew Celia was out with James so she concluded that Rick and Mrs Blake were in bed. She decided to go through to the kitchen and make herself a hot drink, but when she opened the door she found that someone was already there. Over by the sink she could see a figure silhouetted against the window. She gave an involuntary cry of alarm, which was echoed by the figure. There was a crash and Lottie Blake's voice said, 'Now look what you've made me do!'

Gail switched on the light. 'I'm sorry, Mrs Blake. I had no idea anyone was in here. I thought you were a burglar.'

'Burglar, indeed!' Aunt Lottie's voice shook and her face was scarlet as she bent to pick up the pieces of broken glass. 'It's coming to something when one can't walk freely round one's own home without being accused of–'

'I *said* I was sorry,' Gail put in. 'It was just that it was dark, that's all.'

'I don't *have* to put the light on to get a drink, do I?' Aunt Lottie's jaw jutted out challengingly, beads of perspiration stood out on her forehead and her eyes bulged indignantly as she stood up to face Gail. 'I really don't know *what* I shall be expected to put up with next.'

Gail put a hand on the older woman's arm. 'Mrs Blake, please don't get so upset. Is something wrong? Aren't you feeling well?'

'I'm perfectly well!' The denial came out loudly. 'I *told* you. Oh, leave me alone and mind your own business, can't you?' Lottie Blake pushed rudely past and made her way out into the hall, leaving Gail staring after her. There was definitely something wrong, and as the woman had faced her, shouting her defensive words into Gail's face, she had caught her breath – and she was almost certain she knew what her trouble was.

Gail was early arriving at the surgery the following morning. She wanted to have a word with Frances about Fay before the receptionist arrived. In the office she went over to the switchboard to switch calls through to the surgery. Martin had been on call the previous night so calls had been put through to the flat. But when she picked up the receiver she realised that the line was engaged. She was just about to replace it when she recognised Frances's voice at the other end. 'So I didn't get in till five-thirty this morning. Could you and Peter manage

99

if I took the morning off, Martin? Is there anything urgent for me?'

'No, nothing. You get some sleep. I'll call you later,' Martin urged.

Once again Gail started to put the receiver down, but Frances's next words seemed to freeze her arm halfway.

'Martin, have you told the family yet – about *us*, I mean?'

'No – no, I haven't.'

'Don't you think you should?'

'I suppose so. I've been preoccupied with everything else.'

'But they have a right to know. And you know your father would have wanted it.'

At that moment the outer door opened and Madge came in. Gail quickly replaced the receiver, feeling ashamed for having eaves-dropped on a private conversation. Her heart felt like lead. Peter was right, it seemed. They were secretly engaged and clearly Frances was anxious to have it out in the open.

About ten minutes later Martin came down into reception and told her that Frances wouldn't be in that morning.

'A difficult confinement in the early hours,' he explained.

'Can I have a private word?' Gail asked him.

He looked surprised. 'Of course. Come through to the surgery.'

Once inside his room, she explained what

100

had happened the previous evening and about Fay's anxiety.

'I'm fairly certain it's only a small cyst, but I've persuaded her to see Frances this morning. As Frances isn't here, will you see her?' she asked. 'I'm so afraid she'll get cold feet if she has too long to think about it.'

Martin frowned. 'Gail – Fay isn't registered with this practice,' he said. 'She's with old Edgerly, over at Creeton. That's where she used to live. She did ask about changing when she first came to work for us, but I advised her to stay as she was.'

'Couldn't you just look at her – off the record?' Gail asked. 'It's taken her months to pluck up the courage to tell someone. If we send her away now–'

'Gail! You know as well as I do, that would be unethical. Just advise her to go to her own doctor.'

'But couldn't you–'

'*No*, Gail! Strictly speaking you shouldn't have examined her either.'

'But if we're to have a Well Woman Clinic–'

'That's only for our *own* patients,' Martin pointed out. 'We're not a hospital. We can't cope with the entire female population of Lullford. I only wish we could.'

'But if we turn her away she may not go at all!' Gail could hardly contain her impatience. 'This is just the kind of thing that stops women going for these important tests. If we refuse to see them when they *do* come–'

'I'm not refusing, Gail. I'm just asking you to advise Fay to do the ethical thing and go to her own doctor. Look…' He looked at his watch. 'It's almost time for surgery. I can hear patients out there already. And I still have to tell Peter that we're sharing Frances's patients this morning, too.'

Without another word Gail turned and went out, closing the door very firmly behind her. When she had seen Martin with the two injured children she had admired him so much – thought him so caring. How could he be so stubborn over this? Her throat was tight and her eyes stung with tears – tears of anger, frustration and another, more personal emotion that she wasn't prepared to acknowledge.

At lunchtime Gail was shopping in the town when she heard a voice call her name from the other side of the street. Turning she saw Kev Donaghue waving to her. He crossed the road, nipping nimbly between cars, much to the drivers' annoyance.

'You'll get yourself run over,' Gail admonished him as he reached her side.

He grinned. 'Not me. It's great to see you, Gail. What are you doing?'

'Shopping.'

He eyed her parcels. 'Finished? Have you eaten?'

She laughed. 'Yes and no.'

He grabbed her arm and began to steer her firmly along the street. 'Right. I know just the place where we can find a secluded table for two.'

'Wait!' She held back. 'I don't really have time for lunch.'

He paused to look down at her. 'It's very bad for you to skip lunch, you know. How about a pint and a sandwich?'

'Oh, all right, then, a sandwich.' Gail relented. 'As long as it doesn't take more than half an hour.'

'I can tell you my whole life story in half an hour,' he said generously. 'So why are we wasting time?'

Seated at a window table in the Plough, Lullford's oldest coaching inn, in the market square, Kev and Gail ate ploughman's lunches, washed down with the local cider.

'I've been meaning to ring you,' Kev told her. 'I reckon you've settled in enough by now to start thinking about some serious socialising.'

'Not really. My spare time is still taken up with looking for somewhere to live,' Gail said.

He paused, a hunk of crusty bread and cheese halfway to his mouth. 'Well, why didn't you *say* so, for heaven's sake? I can fix you up.'

'You can? Ah, but in what way?' Gail asked suspiciously.

'Well, now – how does a first floor self-contained flat, with *en suite* bathroom sound to you?'

'Wonderful – except that I shouldn't think I'd be able to afford it.'

'It would be to rent, not buy.' Kev mentioned a monthly figure so reasonable that it had Gail staring open-mouthed. 'It's subsidised property, you see,' he explained. 'Mellex-owned. The company bought some large houses and converted them for employees, but they're not as popular as anticipated. I reckon they'd be only too glad to have you take one off their hands.' He grinned mischievously. 'With *me* to vouch for you, that is.'

'Ah but are you sure you could do that?' Gail challenged.

He frowned. 'I'm not too sure about that. I reckon I ought to know you better before I stick my neck out.' His blue eyes twinkled wickedly at her. 'So how about dinner this evening – just for starters?'

Gail laughed. It felt good to laugh and flirt a little. 'All right, Kev,' she said. 'I'd like to have dinner with you this evening.'

'*Great!*' He beamed at her across the table. 'Of course, I knew you wouldn't be able to resist my charisma for long.'

'Don't kid yourself. I'd do anything to get that flat,' Gail told him.

Kev dropped his hand over hers and squeezed it tightly. *'Promises* now, eh?' he whispered, his eyes teasing her. Gail's cheeks flooded with colour and he laughed heartily.

The sound of Kev's big infectious laugh attracted looks of amusement from other customers and, embarrassed, Gail glanced around. Then she saw them: over at the bar Martin and Frances were just being served. Frances was looking in their direction and she waved, leaning over to say something to Martin. But when he turned to look at them Gail saw that he was far from amused. His eyes glittered angrily as they met hers across the room. She paused and her arm, half-lifted to wave, dropped to her side again.

'Shall we go?' she asked Kev quietly. 'I think I'd like to get some fresh air before I go back to the surgery.'

To get to the door they had to pass quite close to where Frances and Martin stood. Frances was still smiling and as Gail passed she said encouragingly, 'Glad to see you've taken my advice.'

Gail glanced at Martin, but he merely nodded a curt acknowledgement to Kev, then turned his back towards her. For the second time that day her chest constricted with pain and resentment. As they made their way through the crowded bar she

105

wished she could have told Martin how unfair and selfish she thought him – how *insensitive*. As they reached the door she felt Kev's hand tighten on her arm and realised she was still staring back to where Martin and Frances stood, deep in conversation. He was looking down at her.

'Coming, love?'

She took a deep breath and forced herself to smile back at him. 'Yes – I'm coming.'

'You OK?' His eyes were kindly as they searched hers.

'Yes – I'm OK.' She swallowed the angry hurt boiling up inside her and followed him out into the street.

CHAPTER SIX

Gail dressed carefully for her date with Kev Donaghue. She applied her make-up and brushed out her hair with an air of near defiance. Martin had shown no interest in taking her out since she had been here in Lullford, so why shouldn't she accept an invitation and start making a social life of her own?

It was a warm evening and she chose a jade-green dress in a soft silky material. With it she wore black patent sandals and carried a matching handbag. Kev had offered to pick her up at Hannerford House but she had tactfully suggested that they met in town. She never had an idea when Martin would appear at the house. Lately he had spent several evenings working in his father's study and she didn't want the awkwardness of running into him with Kev in tow; feeling obliged to explain her movements to him.

She had told Lottie Blake that morning that she wouldn't be in for the evening meal, but the older woman seemed so vague and distant that Gail wondered if she had actually registered the fact. So as she passed

Celia's door on her way out she knocked. At first she thought the other girl must be out and was just about to turn away when the door opened.

'Oh, it's you.' Celia looked pale and her eyes bore the tell-tale signs of weeping. Gail wanted to ask if anything was wrong, but she felt her concern might be construed as nosiness.

'I'm sorry to disturb you. I just wanted to remind you that I'm going to be out for dinner,' she said. 'I did tell Mrs Blake this morning, but I'm not sure if she heard me.'

'She's been in a funny vague mood lately,' Celia agreed. 'I'll remind her for you.' She paused, then said. 'I hope you have a nice evening – Gail.'

'Thanks.' There was something about the way she spoke a kind of wistful appeal. It caused Gail to turn and look at her. 'Are you all right?'

'Yes – *no*. It's James.' Celia's eyes filled with tears. 'We … we had a row. It was horrible. I said some awful things to him. I … I'm afraid it might all be over between us.' Stifling a sob, she turned back into the room. Gail followed, closing the door behind them.

'Oh, please, don't be so upset. It'll work itself out, you'll see.' She slipped an arm round the other girl's heaving shoulders. 'I know how you feel, believe me.'

'*You* do?' Celia's expression of wide-eyed

surprise was hardly flattering, but Gail ignored its implication.

'Men can be thoughtless at times, but anyone can see how much James adores you. He'll be back to make it up before long.'

'You don't know what I said to him,' Celia snuffled.

'I dare say it's pre-wedding nerves,' Gail assured her. 'Everyone gets them, so I'm told. Why don't you give him a ring now and say you're sorry?'

Celia pouted. 'He said some pretty horrid things to me, too,' she said stubbornly. 'I think *he* should be the first. I don't want him to think I'm always going to be the one to give in.' For the first time she looked at Gail properly, registering that she was dressed for an outing. 'I'm sorry. You were going out and I'm holding you up.'

'It's all right. I've plenty of time.'

Celia smiled. 'You look very nice. Is it anyone I know?'

'A man called Kevin Donaghue. He's from the oil company. He's just a friend.'

'Well, I hope he takes you somewhere nice. You deserve it.' Celia produced a handkerchief and blew her nose, looking at Gail apologetically. 'It must have been lonely for you here. We haven't been all that welcoming, have we?'

'You've been very kind,' Gail said. 'It isn't easy, having a stranger in one's home. I think I've found a flat. If I get it I won't have to presume on your kindness much longer.'

'A flat!' Celia sniffed. 'That's what our row was about. I don't know if you knew, but James and I are supposed to be having a flat here at Hannerford House.'

'No, I didn't know. What a good idea,' Gail said.

'I thought so too. The idea was Daddy's. He meant to turn the whole place into flats, one for each of us. The plans were passed and everything. But then he died, and now that Martin is in charge he seems to want to change everything. For some reason he's stopped the builders from starting on the work and the maddening part is, he won't say why. James doesn't seem the slightest bit worried about it. I accused him of having second thoughts about getting married and...'

'Oh, dear. I'm sorry. I suppose Martin has a good reason for holding up the work,' Gail said placatingly.

'In that case, why doesn't he tell us what it is? After all, it's our future he's messing about with!' Celia sighed. 'But I mustn't bother you with it all, especially when you're just off out for the evening.' She paused, looking thoughtfully at Gail. 'If you do leave here, you will keep in touch, won't you?' she said almost shyly.

Gail tried to disguise her surprise. 'Of

course if that's what you'd like.'

'Oh, I would.' Celia smiled. 'And I want you to come to the wedding too. Maybe Martin will bring you.'

'I'd like that very much.'

As she drove into town Gail was thoughtful. It seemed almost as though the members of the Hannerford family lived lives that were totally independent of each other. Patrick seemed a lonely, self-sufficient child, and with Celia's wedding so near she must worry about the delay over the flat. She must miss having a mother to help her and advise her, too. Gail could well imagine how she herself would feel under similar circumstances. And why was Martin being so cagey about his reason for postponing the building work, she wondered?

Kev was waiting when she arrived, standing beside his car in the market place. He wore a smart grey suit with a blue shirt that intensified the colour of his eyes. He looked very handsome. When Gail got out of her car he gave a low whistle. 'Well – I heard all about the English rose type from Ma, but I never thought I'd be lucky enough to find one. You look just great, Gail.'

As she settled herself beside him in the passenger seat of his racy little sports car he said, 'I'll take you to see the flat first, while it's still daylight. Then you can see what you think.'

He drove fast, but skilfully. It was a lovely evening and with the car top down Gail enjoyed the feel of the wind in her hair. In fact she felt more light-hearted than she had since leaving Northbridge. Kev turned to smile at her.

'I like your hair like that. It's softer – more feminine. And that dress is just the colour of your eyes. Anyone ever tell you you're a very pretty lady, Nurse Ingram?'

Gail laughed. At least in Kev's case she *knew* he was flattering.

The houses Mellex had acquired were in a quiet road of Victorian villas on the western side of Lullford.

'I'm told that they were built as guest houses in the town's heyday as a holiday resort.' Kev explained. 'Later they became white elephants. Too big for modern families and too small to turn into the kind of hotels people demand nowadays.' He opened the car door for her. 'But they've converted into quite nice flats, as you'll see.'

Beside the white-painted front door of number sixteen was a row of bells, each with its own slot for the resident's name. Inside they passed through a spacious hall and up the staircase to the first floor. On the landing, a tall window with stained glass caught the last of the day's sunlight, making jewel-coloured reflections on the plain beige carpet. The vacant flat was on the first floor and the moment Gail stepped inside she fell in love with it. Basically it was two large airy rooms, skilfully partitioned to form a tiny bathroom adjoining the bedroom and a compact kitchen cunningly concealed behind folding louvred doors in the living-room. The big bay windows overlooked the tree-lined road outside.

'There's a garden at the back,' Kev explained. 'It's shared by all the tenants. Luckily the caretaker likes gardening and he keeps it in apple-pie order.' He looked at her enquiringly. 'Well – what's the verdict?'

'I love it,' Gail told him with a smile. 'I've only got one question: when can I move in?'

'Next week, if you like. I'll arrange it.' He cleared his throat, looking suddenly sober. 'Er … there's just one thing I haven't told you.'

Gail's heart sank. She might have known there'd be a snag. 'Oh, dear. What's that, Kev?'

'Well – I don't know how particular you are about your neighbours...?'

'I think I'm fairly tolerant … why?'

'Because there's someone here you might not care to live near.'

'Really? Who is it?'

'*Me!*' He grinned.

She laughed with relief. 'Kev!' Don't give me shocks like that. I thought it was Jack the Ripper at least!'

'So you don't feel appalled at the prospect of having yours truly across the landing?'

Her eyes narrowed as she looked at his mischievous face. 'I'm beginning to wonder if I should.'

'Oh, no!' He shook his head. 'I don't give wild parties or play heavy rock records late at night – and I never borrow cups of sugar. And just think – you'll have your own personal watch-dog and bodyguard!'

Gail laughed. 'You *are* an idiot, Kev! All right. I'll take it – watch-dog and all.'

Kev's choice of restaurant was rather different from Martin's. He took her to the Peacock, a trendy place where they specialised in exotic oriental food, and encouraged her to try shark's fin soup and something delicious but unpronounceable that she discovered later was squid. Over the meal he told her about his home in Adelaide and the large family he came from.

'When it came to choosing a career I reckoned engineering would take me anywhere,' he told her. 'So as I'd always wanted to see the world I plumped for that. I've been working in England, for Mellex, for two years, but when this particular project came up I really jumped at it. My great-great-grandfather on my mother's side came from Lullford, you see. He was a fisherman, so Ma used to tell us. He was transported for smuggling. Soon as I get some free time I'm going to try and trace the family.'

'How fascinating, you should ask Martin to help you,' Gail said. 'He was telling me about a little church connected with smuggling where there are smugglers' graves.'

Kev grinned. 'Maybe I'll do that.'

Adjoining the restaurant a disco was in full swing and after their meal Kev asked Gail if she would like to dance.

He threw himself into disco dancing as he did everything else – with rather more enthusiasm and abandon than skill, and Gail found herself helpless with laughter more than once as he threw his long limbs about in time to the music. When she looked at her watch and found that it was almost midnight she was surprised. The evening had flown and she'd really enjoyed herself, but with work tomorrow she decided it was time to make tracks for home. Shouting above the loud music she struggled to make him hear her. *'Time I went home now!'*

He frowned. 'The night's young!' he yelled. 'I was just going to suggest going on to a little club I know.' But her firm refusal soon convinced him. Taking her arm, he steered her though the gyrating crowd, a resigned expression on his face.

Gail found the cool evening air refreshing after the heat and stuffiness of the disco. As Kev helped her into the car he remarked,

'You know you should get out and about more – let your hair down more often. In more than the literal sense, I mean.' He reached out to smooth back the strand of hair that had strayed across her cheek.

She found herself flushing. 'What makes you think I don't?'

'Ah – I can tell.' He looked round at her as he belted himself into the driving seat. 'You're a little – just a *little* inhibited, Gail, my love, if you don't mind my saying so.'

She avoided his frank blue gaze. 'As it happens, I *do* mind.'

There was a pause, then his arm crept round her shoulders. 'Well, that figures. Being inhibited, you would, wouldn't you?'

This piece of logic took a moment to sink in. She lifted her face to his and he seized the opportunity to cup her chin and brush his lips across hers. Very gently Gail pushed him away.

'Some of us prefer to call it caution,' she said.

He laughed gently. 'There's a lot to be said for throwing caution to the winds now and again.'

'Kev!' Gail pulled back from him to look him in the eyes. 'Do you want to make me regret taking the flat opposite yours? I might as well tell you right now that I don't intend to let you railroad me into a relationship.'

He stared at her in mock horror, holding

116

up his hands in surrender. 'Gail! You take things so seriously, girl! It was just a friendly little kiss. No strings. I *like* you. I want us to be friends. That's all.'

'I hope so, Kev,' she told him gravely. 'I do hope so, because I can tell you now that anything else is out of the question.'

'OK. I get the message.' His face relaxed into the familiar good-natured grin. 'But it doesn't stop me wanting to kiss you.' He took her shoulders and pulled her closer, kissing her firmly. 'Who knows,' he said with a wicked glint in his eyes. 'You may even get to like it – in time – in a purely platonic way, of course.'

Some deep instinct told Gail that she could trust Kev. There was something kind and solid about him in spite of the mischievous glint in his eyes. They drove back to the market square in companionable silence. As she was about to get out of the car his hand closed over her arm.

'Gail – no hard feelings?'

She smiled. 'No hard feelings, Kev. I think we understand each other now.'

He nodded thoughtfully. 'One thing I understand,' he said. 'Whoever it is you're carrying that king-sized torch for is some lucky guy. I hope for your sake that he knows it.'

He watched as she got into her car and drove away, a wistful smile on his face. She hadn't denied his assumption that there was someone she cared for. 'Kev Donaghue,' he told himself aloud as he turned the key in the ignition, 'you're a bigger fool than I took you for. And that's saying something!'

When Gail came downstairs the following morning she found Lottie Blake in the kitchen wearing her dressing-gown. She was making herself a cup of tea – and drinking a glass of water while she waited for the kettle to boil.

'Oh, good morning, Mrs Blake. I'm glad I've caught you,' Gail said.

Lottie Blake spun round, her face defensive. *'Caught* me? What do you mean?'

'Just that I have something to tell you,' Gail said. 'I've found a flat, so I'll be moving next week. I'd like to thank you for having me here. You've been very kind.'

'Oh – I see.' Lottie turned away, looking slightly shamefaced. 'I've been nothing of the sort,' she muttered. 'Would you like a cup of tea – Gail?'

Surprised, Gail nodded, sitting down at the kitchen table. 'Thank you, Mrs Blake.' She noticed how thin the older woman was. The dressing-gown she wore hung on her loosely, as though it had been made for a much larger woman. Even in the short time that Gail had known her, Lottie Blake had noticeably lost weight.

'I think I may have got the wrong idea about you,' Lottie said as she poured the tea. 'I've been worried about Martin, you see. He's been under a lot of pressure since his father's death.'

'Why should you think I'd make that worse, Mrs Blake?' Gail asked. 'He did offer me the job here, you know. And I got the impression that I'd be making things easier for him, not harder.'

'Of course. It's just...' Lottie bit her lip and looked hesitantly at Gail. 'I wondered if you and he... He'd been away from us for quite a time, and...' She cleared her throat and took a long thoughtful drink of tea. 'There's always been an understanding between him and Frances, you see.' She smiled. 'Well, of course, you'll have seen it for yourself now that Frances is back again. One has only to look at the two of them together to see the way things are.'

'And you were afraid I'd spoil that?' Gail swallowed hard at the knot in her throat.

Lottie nodded. 'You're a very pretty girl. And young men are – well, *young men*. But I know now that you're a sensible and mature young woman and wouldn't do anything to spoil Martin's future.'

'Of course not.' Gail couldn't begin to understand Lottie Blake's reasoning. Surely Martin would make his own choice, so how could *she* do anything to spoil things for him? She drank the last of her tea and stood up. 'I'll have to be going now, Mrs Blake–' She stopped as the older woman suddenly clasped a hand to her throat and gasped, beads of sweat breaking out on her forehead. *'Mrs Blake!* Are you all right? What is it?'

'It's – these palpitations,' Lottie gasped. 'It'll pass off in a minute.'

'You're not really very well, are you?' Gail lifted one of the thin wrists and felt for the pulse. It was fast and irregular. 'Why haven't you mentioned it to anyone – Martin, for instance?'

Lottie shook her head. 'It's nothing. I wouldn't dream of worrying him. The poor boy has enough on his plate at the moment. I'm not getting any younger. I suppose I must expect these things.'

'Nevertheless, I think you should see someone. Would you like me to speak to him about it?'

Lottie got hurriedly to her feet. 'No! Please don't. I told you, I'm quite all right. If I need help, I'll ask for it!'

The message was loud and clear. *Don't interfere,* Lottie Blake's manner reverted to her normal stiff formality as she straightened her back. 'You'd better go now. You'll be late for surgery.'

With a sigh, Gail turned away. It gave her a frustrated feeling of helplessness when a patient refused assistance, but in Lottie

Blake's case she was deeply uneasy. As the older woman had turned towards her she had caught her breath again – the unmistakable odour of apples. She knew that without help she could be seriously ill. Like it or not, Lottie must have help and soon.

The first Well Woman Clinic took place on the following Wednesday afternoon. Fay had agreed to come in on clinic afternoons to help with the filling in of the necessary forms. She had arranged for a friend to pick her children up from school. But Gail noticed that she was quiet as she went about her job. She wondered if the receptionist had taken her advice and made an appointment with her own doctor.

They were busy during the two hours the clinic was open and afterwards Frances was pleased. 'I think most of the patients were impressed with the informal, relaxed atmosphere,' she said as she changed out of her white coat in Gail's room. 'Not to say relieved that the examinations are painless.'

Gail turned, about to ask if Fay had mentioned her own worry, but the words she was about to say were forgotten as she faced Frances. It was a warm afternoon and the other girl had worn only her slip under the white coat. As she stepped into her green linen dress and began to button it, Gail caught sight of a fine gold chain around her neck. From it hung a diamond ring. She averted her eyes, busying herself with the forms on her desk. *Why would anyone wear a ring around their neck where no one could see it?* There was only one answer – a secret engagement.

After Frances had left Gail packed the samples ready to be taken to the laboratory, while Fay carefully filed the forms.

'Did you see Dr Edgerly as I suggested?' Gail asked as they worked.

Fay shook her head. 'I haven't had time yet.'

'You really should go soon,' Gail told her. 'When I suggested that Dr Grant would see you I didn't realise you weren't a patient here, but you shouldn't let that stop you.'

Fay smiled. 'I won't. But I do wish Dr Edgerly would start a clinic like this. It would make it all much easier.'

Apart from seeing him briefly at the surgery, Gail hadn't seen Martin to speak to since the day she'd had lunch with Kev at the Plough, but that night, as she turned her car into the drive at Hannerford House, she saw through her rear-view mirror that he was following her. He pulled up behind her in front of the house and she got out of the car to find herself facing him.

'Hello, Gail. How did the clinic go this afternoon?'

She found her heart quickening as she looked into his eyes. 'Fine. We were kept busy for the full two hours. I think it's going to be a success.' She started to go up the steps but he reached out to touch her arm. 'Gail – Aunt Lottie tells me you're leaving.'

'Yes.' She turned to look at him. 'I think it's best. I've been lucky enough to find a flat. Staying here was only meant to be a temporary measure after all, wasn't it?'

'You were lucky to find somewhere. Where is it?'

She found herself unable to meet his searching eyes. 'It's over on the other side of Lullford – Hemmingbury Road.'

His brows came together. 'Those are Mellex houses!'

'Yes, as a matter of fact.'

He regarded her for a moment. 'Would Kev Donaghue have anything to do with this?'

'He put me on to it, yes.'

'Have you been seeing him?' Martin's smile had vanished and Gail felt her anger rise.

'We've been out to dinner – if it's any of your business.'

'I hope you know what you're getting into, Gail.'

'I'm not *getting into* anything – except a new flat!'

'I suppose you know that Donaghue lives

123

in the same road?'

'He lives in the same house, as it happens,' she told him defiantly. 'Right across the landing.' She looked at him levelly, her eyes blazing. It was on the tip of her tongue to make a remark about it making a change to have a friendly neighbour, but she stopped herself just in time. With an exasperated little cry she turned away, but Martin caught her arm and held it fast.

'Gail! I want to talk to you. Look, let's go for a walk.'

She wanted to ask what there was to talk about. She certainly didn't feel at home here at Hannerford House. Her attempts to help were interpreted as interference. He was secretly engaged to Frances. It would be better if she had never come to Lullford – better if they had never *met*. But as she opened her mouth to say so she caught the expression in his dark eyes and her anger evaporated. Instead she said, 'All right. Why not?'

They crossed the garden in silence and went through the gate to the cliff path. As they began to descend Gail caught her toe in a root and stumbled. Martin caught her arm, pulling her against his side.

'Steady!' As their eyes met he asked, 'Gail, you are happy here, aren't you?'

'Of course,' she said unconvincingly.

'You don't regret leaving Northbridge –

your old job?'

'No.' The monosyllable echoed feebly inside her head, a betrayal of all she was really feeling. But her heart was so full of questions clamouring to be answered that she didn't know where to begin. He was so different here. The carefree, debonair Dr Martin Hannerford might have been a figment of her imagination. Here, in his own environment, he was sober and preoccupied – almost unapproachable at times. Why did you pretend you felt more for me than you did? she longed to ask. Why don't you tell people that you and Frances are to be married, when it seems to be the one thing they all expect and want? A sigh escaped her and he stopped walking to pull her round to face him, his dark eyes searching hers.

'I hoped we'd see more of each other than we have, Gail, but things haven't turned out in quite the way we hoped, have they?'

'I don't think I've ever known what you hoped, Martin.' Her voice trembled and she tried to break free, but his grip on her shoulders tightened.

'Don't!' His eyes burned into hers. 'Things are more complicated than I expected. It's impossible to explain for the time being. I would like to hear what you really feel though, Gail. I'd like to think you could still talk to me.'

How *could* he say that? What was she

supposed to say? It was all so unfair. She shook her head, swallowing hard at the knot of tears in her throat. 'I don't *know* what I feel any longer, Martin. Except that I was stupid and naïve – that I should never have come here.'

'I was afraid you might be feeling like that.' He lifted her chin, his hand hard and unrelenting as he forced her to look at him. 'All I ask is that you trust me – just for a little longer.' Before she could reply his mouth covered her trembling lips, tenderly coaxing them into submission, his arms drawing her closer till her body was moulded to his. The kiss seemed endless as he slowly and un-remittingly broke down her resistance. Their lips parted momentarily, then met again, this time eagerly and passionately. When at last Martin let her go she was trembling.

Martin's voice was husky as he held her close. His hand cradled her head against his shoulder. 'Surely you know why I asked you to come here, Gail? But since then so much has happened. There are complications that I can't go into now. Do you understand?'

But Gail was only more confused than ever. All she knew for sure was that she was more deeply in love with him than ever. She longed to ask about Frances but before she was able to a twig snapped close by and the bushes parted to reveal a small grubby red-faced figure. Martin's arms dropped abruptly to his sides as he stared at his young brother.

'*Rick!* What the devil–?'

'I wasn't spying. Honestly! I never *meant* to listen!'

'Go to your room at once!' Martin shouted. 'I'll speak to you later. The sooner September is here and you're off to Langthorpe School, the better!'

The boy scuttled away and Gail looked at Martin. 'Poor Rick. I'm sure he didn't mean to.'

He sighed. 'I know he didn't. His trouble is that no one here really has time to give him the attention he deserves. It isn't his fault, poor kid. He's off to boarding school in the autumn term. It seemed the only answer, under the circumstances.'

Gail had seen the look of misery on Rick's face when the school was mentioned. 'Does he really have to go?' she asked. 'Isn't there any other way?'

'Not really,' he said. 'Anyway, it's what Father always intended for him. He took out an insurance to make sure of it when Rick was born, just in case he didn't live long enough to see him grow up.' He took her hand. 'Gail, will you come to the flat this evening? At least we'll have privacy to talk there. There's so much I have to explain to you.'

'I'll come,' she promised happily. Maybe at last she could ask all the questions that she longed to ask – find a solution to the web of secrecy that seemed to surround the Hannerford family.

CHAPTER SEVEN

Dinner that evening was a quiet meal. Celia did not appear and Gail had no idea whether she was still upset or whether she had made up her quarrel with James and gone out. Aunt Lottie seemed preoccupied and Rick was pale and quiet, pushing his food round his plate in a desultory way until Martin admonished him.

'Eat up your food properly, Rick. Aunt Lottie has taken a lot of trouble to cook it for you.'

Rick's lower lip trembled and he pushed his chair back from the table. 'Well she won't have to for much longer, will she?' he burst out. 'You'll all soon be rid of me.' He ran from the room and even though Martin commanded him to come back and apologise he could he heard running up the stairs. Aunt Lottie looked at Martin.

'Why can't you let the child go to the local grammar school?' she asked. 'He did get a place there. I don't agree with sending children away.'

'He'll enjoy it once he gets used to it,' Martin said firmly. 'After all, it is one of the best schools in the country.'

'*You* weren't sent to a boarding school,' she reminded him.

'I had two parents,' Martin reminded her. 'You know Father made provision for Rick, knowing he probably wouldn't be here to see him finish his education.'

'I'm here,' Lottie pointed out.

'You've done your share of looking after us all, Aunt Lottie. Now it's time you had a little peace. And however much we might want to, the rest of us just haven't the time to devote to Rick.'

Lottie Blake's shoulders slumped and Gail couldn't make up her mind whether it was because she knew she couldn't win an argument with Martin, or whether she was forced to agree with him. She suspected the latter. But her heart went out to Rick. He was such a lovable child. It must seem like the end of the world to him to be leaving his home and family, everything that was familiar, especially so soon after the death of his father.

Martin left as soon as the meal was over, taking a briefcase full of papers from his father's study with him. On her way upstairs to change Gail paused outside Rick's bedroom door. Making up her mind, she tapped on it. 'Rick – may I come in?'

'If you like,' came the muffled reply.

She found him sprawled on the floor, moodily examining his collection of fossils.

'Would you like to talk?' she asked.

He raised himself on one elbow, regarding her suspiciously. 'Did Martin send you to tell me off for being rude?'

'No.' She sat on the edge of his bed. 'Rick, I know how you feel. When I was about your age, my parents were divorced and I had to leave my home and go and live with an aunt. It feels like the end of the world at the time, but it isn't. It's just the beginning of a new life – maybe an exciting one.'

He looked unconvinced. 'I just want to stay here. I want everything to stay the same.' He looked up at her appealingly. 'I wish Martin *would* marry you!'

'Why do you say that?'

'Because Frances is a doctor. She'd be too busy to stay at home and keep house.'

'And you think I would?' Gail couldn't help smiling. Children's motives were so guilelessly selfish. As Martin had said, at least one knew where one was with Rick. She felt she owed him the same honesty.

'Rick, I think you've got to face the fact that Martin is head of the family now and what he has chosen for all of you is for your own good.'

'But – you do want to marry him, don't you?'

'Even grown-up people don't always get what they want, Rick. It isn't very likely.'

Rick sat up, frowning. 'But this afternoon

131

– you and he – you were *kissing!* I thought that usually meant–' He broke off as Gail shook her head.

'You mustn't jump to conclusions. People are more complicated than that. Things aren't always what they seem.'

Pulling a face he slumped back, folding his arms. 'I'll never understand grown-ups,' he said dejectedly. 'They do such *barmy* things!'

And although she didn't say so, Gail was inclined to agree with him. She stood up. 'I've got to go now, but you can always talk to me if you get fed up.'

He looked at her. 'I can't if you're not here, can I? You're leaving too!'

Gail bit her lip. It was true of course. The poor child must feel that everyone was deserting him. 'You can come to tea,' she told him. 'If you've got a piece of paper and a pencil I'll leave you my telephone number, then you can call me any time you like. I'll come over in the car and fetch you. How's that?'

His face brightened as he scrambled to his feet to fetch paper and pencil for her. 'Can I? Wow, great! Thanks, Gail.'

She felt better as she went to her room to change. Rick's unhappiness reminded her so poignantly of her own hurt and bewilderment at the collapse of her parents' marriage. And she reflected that the pain of rejection hurt no less however many years had passed. The only difference was that the older one was, the harder it was to share the unhappiness. What was it that Martin was so anxious to tell her this evening? she wondered.

She changed into a pair of pale grey corduroy jeans, teamed with a cerise sweater, applied fresh make-up and picked up her car keys and the keys to the surgery. The house was silent as she made her way downstairs. There was still no sign of Celia.

Parking the car in the small car park at the rear of the surgery, Gail made her way round to the front entrance and let herself in with her own key. The flat was reached by going through the office to a staircase at the back. But as Gail reached the landing she saw that the door to the flat was ajar and voices came from inside. Martin was not alone. She hesitated – then she heard a familiar feminine voice and realised that Martin's visitor was Frances. Her voice was raised and she questioned Martin impatiently.

'Haven't you told the family yet?'

'No.'

'Oh, Martin! For heaven's sake, why not? They'll have to know soon.'

'When Father's solicitor gets back from this extended holiday he's having we can get everything sorted out,' he told her. 'Till then

I'd rather keep it between you and me.'

'I want it out in the open now, Martin,' Frances insisted. 'All this secrecy is ruining things for me. Deciding to marry is the most important decision I've ever made. Why should I have to keep it quiet?'

'You must realise that there's more at stake than putting that ring on your finger, Frances. I know how important it is to you. Believe me, I want it all to be open and above board too. But I must see Father's solicitor before we make any more plans. Can you just be patient till then, please?'

'I suppose I'll have to.' Frances paused. 'Have you mentioned it to Gail?'

'Not so far. I've asked her to look in here this evening.'

'Then I think you should take the opportunity to let her in on it.' Frances told him quietly. 'She's in love with you, Martin. You must know that. I think we owe it to her to tell her.'

Gail stood motionless on the staircase, her face hot with humiliation. So she had been right. They were engaged and Martin had intended to tell her so tonight. Had he tried to let her down lightly this afternoon with his kisses and his hints about complications and trust? She turned and slipped silently down the stairs again.

She couldn't wait to get away from the building. It would be so embarrassing if they knew she had overheard their conversation. Desperately anxious not to be discovered, her fingers fumbled clumsily with the door catch as she attempted to let herself out silently.

The next few minutes were occupied with putting as much distance as she could between herself and the surgery, but halfway back to Hannerford House she stopped the car at the side of a quiet road and forced herself to think rationally about the conversation she had overheard. Obviously, for some reason concerning Martin's father's will, his engagement to Frances would not be announced yet. That much was clear. But that being the case, why had he kissed her this afternoon, and led her to believe that he cared for her?

She slept badly that night, tossing and turning – dreaming in troubled, confused snatches. She woke late, feeling weary, with a dull pain pounding relentlessly behind her eyes.

When she arrived at the surgery Frances was waiting for her in her room.

'Ah, Gail. Can I have a word? It's about Fay. She's just told me about this lump that's worrying her so much. She tells me you knew about it, and that you promised to ask me to look at it. Why didn't you tell me?'

'It was the morning you missed surgery,'

Gail explained. 'I asked Martin to see her instead. I thought Fay might get cold feet if it was postponed for too long. But he said that the Well Woman Clinic facilities were for our own patients only.'

Frances frowned. 'You mean he refused to see her?'

'He said it would be unethical. I hadn't realised she wasn't on our list.'

'But it's so easy to change now,' Frances insisted. 'Didn't you point that out to her?'

'No. I didn't see it as my job to tell her she should change. I just advised her to make an appointment with her own doctor.'

'But she didn't, did she?'

'Apparently not.'

Frances shook her head. 'I do wish you'd mentioned it to me, Gail. She's been worrying herself silly ever since. I could have saved her so much anxiety. You see, she heard yesterday that a close friend of hers has had a radical mastectomy. It terrified her. She hasn't slept all night. She looks like nothing on earth this morning. I've told her I'll see her immediately after surgery and I'd like you to be there too.'

'But what about Dr Edgerly?' Gail asked.

'He doesn't do a women's clinic. Fay is changing to this practice today. She can easily do that under the new ruling.' Frances was halfway through the door when she turned. 'She'd have to shortly, anyway. Dr

Edgerly is retiring next year.'

Gail felt annoyed and resentful. It was Martin's fault really, so why blame her?

On her way to the office to pick up her patients' cards for the morning she ran into Martin in the corridor. Her cheeks burning, she made to hurry past, but he caught her arm.

'Gail! What happened last night? You didn't come.'

'It's no use, Martin. I *know*,'she said, facing him. 'About you and Frances, I mean. So there's nothing more to say.'

He looked mystified. 'You *know?* But how–?'

'It doesn't matter how I know. The important thing is that I do. Please let me go. I don't want to discuss it any further.' She shook her arm free.

'Gail! Come back here. I–'

'Good morning. Everything all right?' Hearing their raised voices, Peter Shires had come out of his room and was looking curiously from one to the other. With an exasperated snort Martin turned and went into his room, slamming the door behind him.

'Well!' Peter looked at Gail's flushed face. 'Are you all right?'

'Yes.' Gail took a deep breath and turned away before he could see the tears in her eyes. The day that had begun so badly was obviously not destined to improve.

After the last patient had been seen Frances asked Fay and Gail into her room. She examined Fay and agreed that she should be referred to a consultant as soon as possible. Picking up the telephone, she rang the hospital herself and managed to get an appointment for the following week.

'They don't keep you waiting for this kind of thing,' she explained to Fay.

'Does that mean it's serious?' Fay asked fearfully, buttoning her blouse again.

'It's important that anything of this kind is looked at as soon as possible,' Frances told her. 'Anyway, I'm sure you'd rather get it over with.'

'Of course. I just wish it were over now.'

'Is there anyone who could go with you?' Gail asked her.

'No.' Fay shook her head firmly. 'I'd rather do this alone. I'll break the news when I have some to break – good or bad.'

Frances patted her arm. 'Well, just remember the statistics. The odds against it being anything nasty are ninety-nine point nine per cent. And those are long odds in anyone's book.'

'I'll try and remember.' Fay smiled. 'Thanks anyway, both of you.'

When she had gone Frances looked at Gail. 'Sorry I blew my top a bit this morning,' she said. 'I've seen Martin since and he tells me it was all his fault. He was rather preoccupied that morning. He says he was probably a bit short with you over it.' She grinned ruefully. 'And then I had to start on you too. I'm sorry.'

'That's all right. It's par for the course today,' Gail said. 'It's turning out to be one of those days.'

'Join the club!' Frances said. She looked closely at Gail. 'Is anything wrong – that I can help with, I mean? You look a bit under the weather yourself.'

Gail shook her head. Frances was the very last person to help under the circumstances. Besides, she already knew too much about her for comfort.

'A headache, that's all. I didn't sleep very well last night,' she said. 'I'm moving into my new flat on Saturday. I dare say it's excitement.'

On Saturday mornings the surgery was open for emergencies only, with Gail and one doctor on duty. The following Saturday was busier than usual. There seemed to be a constant stream of cuts and bruises, neg-lected colds that had suddenly turned into bronchitis, and more than the usual number of home accidents. Gail was kept busy all morning, dressing lacerations and treating sprains and abrasions. Surgery was almost over when she found a middle-aged couple sitting in the waiting-room. The man sheepishly escorted his wife into Gail's room.

'She's hurt her arm,' he said. 'Climbing a ladder. I told her not to but would she wait–?'

The woman snorted. 'If I waited for him to do these jobs they'd never get done!' She sniffed and looked at Gail. 'It's nothing much, just a sprain or something. I didn't want to come, only *he* made me.' She gave her husband another baleful look.

Gail helped the woman remove her blouse, but when the arm was lifted she let out a sharp cry and her face drained of colour.

'It's all right,' Gail said. 'Just rest there for a moment.'

She went out into the corridor and put her head round Martin's room. 'I've got a patient with a DIY injury,' she told him. 'I'm afraid it might be a fractured humerus. Would you come and have a look?'

Examining the woman carefully, Martin agreed with Gail's diagnosis. 'How did it happen?' he asked. 'What were you doing?'

She shot her husband a look. 'I was on the roof,' she announced. 'Fixing the TV aerial. It's weeks since that set went on the blink. Ruined all my favourite programmes. It was like trying to look at *Dynasty* through a thick fog!' She glared at her erring spouse. 'But *would* he fix it? Would he 'ell! Asked him till I was blue in the face. So in the end I decided to try and fix it myself – and now look at me!'

'Well, I hope you succeeded, because I'm afraid you're going to need that television now. You'll be out of action for quite some time, I'm afraid,' Martin warned her. 'I'd like you to go along to the hospital for X-rays. They'll make you as comfortable as possible.'

While Gail immobilised the patient's arm he sat down at her desk to write a note. The woman looked at Gail as she fastened the sling.

'*Men!*' she said scathingly. 'Well, he'll have *everything* to do now and I hope he likes it!' She glared at her unhappy-looking husband. 'Perhaps you'll let this be a lesson to you!'

When the pair had gone Gail looked at Martin and they exchanged a grin. 'Poor bloke,' Martin remarked. 'Unless I'm very much mistaken, he's in for a tough time.' He shook his head. 'It's hard to imagine those two were once a pair of starry-eyed young lovers, isn't it?'

'Almost impossible!' Gail chuckled. 'Life plays some strange practical jokes at times, doesn't it?'

His eyes held hers. 'Some cruel ones at times. Gail – I meant to ask you to have lunch today but I have an urgent trip to make this afternoon. I have a patient to see first. I'd rather like you to meet her. Will you come with me.'

Miss Henshaw was eighty-seven and almost crippled with arthritis. Her cottage was on the quay, just a few doors away from where Frances lived. In the sunny little living-room, a canary sang sweetly in its cage near a window that overlooked the harbour with its bobbing boats. When Martin walked in she looked up from her chair, greeting him with a welcoming smile.

'Oh, it's you, Doctor. I was hoping you'd come today. I'm almost out of my pills and I didn't like to bother you at the weekend.'

Martin shook his head at her. 'You know you can ring me at any time,' he told her. 'I knew you must have almost finished them so I've brought you a supply from the dispensary.' He put the box on the mantel-piece and turned to Gail. 'I've brought my new practice nurse to meet you. She used to be a community nurse and she has had a lot of patients like you.'

The old lady was delighted to have a new visitor and insisted on making coffee for the three of them. They sat chatting for half an hour or so and when at last they said good-bye and left the cottage Martin turned to Gail. 'Miss Henshaw looked after her invalid parents until she was almost fifty,' he told her. 'There was a man in her life – a fisherman. He waited thirty years for her to be free to marry. But just a few weeks before the wedding his boat went down and he was lost at sea.'

'Oh. Poor Miss Henshaw.'

Martin sighed. 'We should take all the happiness we can while it's there to take.' His voice was tight and when she looked at him she saw the lines of strain around his mouth. It was almost as though he felt a special affinity with the old lady and she wondered why.

'I agree,' she whispered.

Suddenly he sighed and looked at her. 'Gail – things aren't always what they seem. I don't know why you didn't come to the flat the other night – or what it is you think you know. At the moment I'm not in a position to explain things fully. All I ask is that you trust me for just a little longer.'

She looked at him, her mind seething with questions, but the look in his eyes seemed to melt her intention to ask them. 'If you say so,' she said quietly.

He took her hand as she was getting into her car. 'After today it could all be over,' he said.

She drove to the end of the quay to turn her car, but as she was driving back she saw Frances come out of her cottage and wave to Martin. She was elegantly dressed in a cream linen suit and she didn't see Gail as she climbed into the car beside Martin. But Gail had seen the eager happiness on her face as she passed. *An urgent trip to make,* Martin had said. He hadn't said that Frances was going too!

She was packing the last of her cases into the car later that afternoon when Celia came running up. 'Oh, good. I was afraid I'd miss you,' she said. 'I wanted you to have this before you go.' She held out a large envelope.

Gail opened it to find it was a wedding invitation. She looked up with a smile. 'So it's all on again, then?'

The other girl smiled. 'Yes, we made it up. I'm sure you were right about wedding nerves. I'm certain everything will be all right once the wedding is over.'

'I hadn't realised it was so soon.' Gail looked at the invitation. 'Only a couple of weeks away. No wonder you were worried about the flat.'

'It's all right now. James has found us a house to rent,' Celia told her happily. 'Some friends of his have gone abroad for two years. They've said we can have their house for as long as we need it.' She smiled. 'We've been spending a bit of time there – moving in some of our own things. And we're going away today for the weekend, just the two of us. We've both agreed that we need some time to ourselves.'

144

'That's marvellous. And thank you for inviting me. I shall look forward to it very much.'

'I'm afraid all the preparations have been a strain for Aunt Lottie,' Celia confided. 'We're having the reception at a hotel, so she hasn't had any catering to think about, but she looks so tired all the time. I think she's lost weight too.'

'So you've noticed, too? Where is she, by the way?' Gail asked. 'I'd like to say goodbye to her.'

'She said she had a sore throat. She couldn't eat any lunch so I suggested she should go and lie down. But I'll tell her you said goodbye.'

As she drove out through the gates, Gail sighed a little wistfully. She'd expected to be glad to leave Hannerford House behind her, yet since she'd found the flat her relationship with Martin's family had undergone a change. Could *she* possibly have been the one to misjudge?

Gail worked steadily for the rest of the afternoon and by six o'clock the flat looked almost like home, and her empty cases were stowed away in the cupboard under the stairs that Kev had shown her. She was just about to make herself a snack when the telephone ran. She picked up the receiver wondering who could possibly be ringing her so soon.

'Hello. Gail Ingram here.'

'Gail. It's me – Rick.'

'*Rick*. Is anything wrong?'

'Yes, it's Aunt Lottie.' The boy's voice was tight with fear. 'We were playing Scrabble just now and she started to look all funny. Then she just sort of folded up and fell off her chair. I can't get her to wake up, Gail I tried to get Martin but he isn't in the flat.'

'Have you tried Frances?'

'She's not in either.'

Gail remembered that Peter Shires was on call. Martin and Frances were probably out together somewhere. 'I'm on my way,' she told him. 'Listen, Rick, have you got Dr Shires' number?'

'Yes.'

'Well ring him and ask him to come over right away. Say I said so. And get a blanket and cover Aunt Lottie up to keep her warm.'

To make sure, she rang both Martin and Frances again, but there was still no reply to either number. On her way out she knocked on Kev's door. 'I've got to go back to Hannerford House,' she told him. 'Mrs Blake has collapsed. It could be serious. I've left messages for Martin and Frances. If either of them should ring would you tell them?' She handed him her key.

It was only about two miles across town to Hannerford House but Gail found herself held up in the early evening traffic. When she got there she found an anxious Rick standing on the steps.

'How is she?' she asked him.

'She still hasn't woken up.' He looked close to tears. 'You've been an awful long time. I thought you weren't coming.'

'Did you get hold of Dr Shires?' Gail was hurrying through the hall.

'Yes. He's coming.'

Gail found Lottie Blake lying on the drawing-room floor. Bending over her she sniffed and found the smell of apples almost overwhelming. She hesitated. For all she knew Lottie might have already sought help. Her symptoms could be due to lack of insulin or an excess of it. Looking round she found Lottie's handbag and began to search through the contents. She could find no tablets or ampoules – no steroid card. Their existence would have been a help, but the fact that she found none proved nothing. There was still no sign of Peter Shires and she knew she must make a decision – quickly. Celia had said that her aunt had a sore throat – and that she hadn't eaten any lunch. Everything pointed to low insulin. She looked up.

'Rick. Go to the telephone and dial 999. Ask them to send an ambulance urgently and make sure you give them the address correctly.'

As the boy left the room, Lottie groaned slightly and Gail looked down to see her eyelids fluttering. She seemed to be coming round. Thank God she'd only lost consciousness and hadn't dropped into a coma. As Rick came back into the room, she said 'Run to the kitchen and get me a glass of warm water. Stir a big teaspoonful of sugar into it and bring it here as quickly as you can.'

A few minutes later he was back. Gail held the glass to Lottie's lips, raising her head.

'Try to drink this, Mrs Blake. Everything's going to be fine. We'll soon have you better again.'

Lottie drank the sugared water thirstily. But after a few moments she still seemed drowsy.

Rick jumped up. 'I can hear Dr Shires' car! I'll go and let him in.'

Peter looked flushed as he came into the room. 'Sorry I took so long – damned traffic.' He crouched down beside Lottie. 'What's the trouble?'

'Hyperglycaemia,' Gail told him briskly. 'I'm not surprised, from what I've seen since I've been here. I've given her some sugared water but there's been no dramatic improvement, so it looks as though she wasn't under treatment.'

Peter made a brief examination. 'I've certainly never heard Martin mention that his aunt was diabetic,' he said. 'Better get her to a hospital as soon as possible.'

'We've already sent for an ambulance,' Rick put in. 'And I think I can hear it coming now.'

Gail waited at the cottage hospital while Lottie Blake was admitted. A pale-faced Rick sat beside her in the waiting-room.

'She will be all right, won't she, Gail?' he whispered, his hand creeping into hers.

She gave his hand a reassuring squeeze. 'Thanks to you, she will. You were a very good boy to act so promptly.' She was thinking of all the things that might have happened. Lottie's collapse was more than likely due to the sore throat she had been complaining of. Lack of insulin was often aggravated by an infection, and the fact that she hadn't eaten would be enough to tip the balance. She could have passed into a deep coma while she was resting on her bed this afternoon, and lain there undiscovered until it was too late to help. She shuddered, wishing she had alerted Martin or Frances when her suspicions were first aroused.

Peter reappeared and Gail stood up as he came into the room.

'How is she?'

'She's stable now. You can slip in and see her if you like,' he said. 'She's on a drip for the time being and we'll have to keep her in for a day or two, but once her diabetes is under proper management she'll be fine.' He shook his head. 'She must have been feeling rotten for some time. If only she'd asked one of us for help.'

'Doctors' families all too often get overlooked,' Gail observed. 'Peter...' She glanced down at Rick. 'I must try and get hold of Martin as soon as possible. I've rung both his number and Frances's. They're both out but I have left messages. I'd like to hang on in case they arrive, to explain what happened, but–'

'Rick can come with me,' Peter said, anticipating her worry. 'With a bit of luck I won't get called out again, but if I do he can always come along and wait in the car. We can have a game of chess, eh, old man?'

Rick stood up, looking happier. 'Yes, please.'

'I'll pick you up at Peter's later and you'd better come home with me,' Gail told the boy. 'You can't stay on your own with Celia away for the weekend.'

Up in the ward the Sister gave Gail permission to sit with Lottie for a while. The older woman looked a little better now that she was on the glucose drip. She even managed to smile as Gail pulled a chair up beside the bed.

'I have to thank you, my dear,' she said.

'They tell me I owe my life to your prompt action.'

Gail shook her head. 'It was Rick really. He rang me when you collapsed.'

Lottie frowned, turning her head from side to side on the pillow. 'I hate to be so much trouble. I *loathe* illness. I always have.'

'But it doesn't go away if you ignore it,' Gail told her gently. 'And you have been trying to ignore it, haven't you?'

Lottie nodded. 'I'm afraid I have.' To Gail's surprise the older woman reached out for her hand. 'Will you do something for me? I *must* see Frances – as soon as possible.'

'I've already left messages for both Frances and Martin,' Gail told her. 'I'm sure they'll be along to see you as soon as they get them.'

'It's Frances I must see, though – *alone*. It's very important.' Her hand clutched Gail's convulsively. 'There's something I have to tell her, you see – and *soon*.' She looked at Gail, her eyes troubled. 'This ... this diabetes; it's hereditary, isn't it?'

'It can be, but it's by no means inevitable. Why?'

Lottie's voice dropped so low that Gail had to bend close to the bed to hear what she was saying.

'Because Frances is mine – *my* child. I'm her mother,' Lottie whispered. 'It was because of that that I did what I did. And

151

now I'm afraid I may have upset everyone's life – including hers. If I have, I'll never, *never* forgive myself.'

CHAPTER EIGHT

'Please, Mrs Blake, don't upset yourself,' Gail said soothingly. For an instant she wondered if Lottie could be feverish. She seemed to be talking in riddles. She was certainly confused. But the older woman seemed to need to unburden herself now that she had started to talk.

'Not many people know that I was married a second time,' she said quietly. 'I was in my mid-thirties when I met Danny Grant. He was several years younger than me but he swept me completely off my feet.'

She sighed. 'There'd been no one else since my dear Paul was killed. I was only eighteen then and we had so little time together. By the time I met Danny I was old enough to have known better, but he was so attractive and witty. He made me laugh, and that was something I'd almost forgotten how to do.'

Gail pressed the hand that still lay in hers. 'Mrs Blake – I really don't think you should be telling all this to me – a stranger.'

But Lottie shook her head. 'They'll all have to know soon, so it doesn't matter.' She smiled at Gail. 'Anyway, you're not a stranger, dear. You care a great deal for Martin, don't you? I've seen that for myself and for that reason all this concerns you too.' She drew a deep breath and continued her story. 'Danny and I had only been married six months when he suddenly disappeared. I thought he'd left me, but I soon found out that the police were after him. He'd been embezzling money from the firm he worked for. They caught up with him in the end, of course, and eventually he went for trial. He was found guilty and sentenced to five years' imprisonment.' She looked at Gail, her eyes dark with remembered pain. 'By that time our baby – Frances – had been born. But then came the worst blow of all. I discovered that we'd never been legally married. Danny already had a wife in Ireland.'

Gail gasped. 'Oh, poor Mrs Blake. What did you do?'

'I didn't know which way to turn. I had no money and no home. Danny had spent every penny we had in our joint account and I'd mortgaged the house to pay for his lawyer during the trial. When John and Margaret – Martin's parents – offered to take my baby, I had little choice but to accept. Margaret only had Martin then and she'd always wanted a little girl. At least it meant I wouldn't lose touch with Frances. Later, when Margaret died after having Patrick, I saw my chance to return their kindness and be with my daughter at the same time.' Lottie smiled wanly. 'The rest you know.'

'And you never told Frances?' To Gail it seemed incredible that Lottie could have kept the secret all these years.

'No. I'd promised Margaret, you see. She'd always loved Frances as her own child – even after Celia was born. By the time I came back into Frances's life she was in her teens. It seemed too late, so I decided to keep quiet.' She looked at Gail hesitantly. 'But now she has to know. It's only fair isn't it – because of this illness?'

It seemed to Gail that there was a much deeper need for Lottie to tell Frances the truth about her birth; perhaps one that even she herself didn't care to acknowledge. Gail felt it wasn't her place to advise.

'I always wanted to see Frances and Martin marry,' Lottie was saying. 'All the time they were growing up together it seemed inevitable that they would fall in love. They were always so close. It was my dearest wish – it became almost an obsession. But then Martin went to Northbridge and I wasn't so sure any more. When he came home I sensed a change in him. I suppose I panicked. Then I had the idea. I talked John into doing it. But now I wish I hadn't.'

Gail had no idea what Lottie had made her late brother do, but whatever it was, the thought of it seemed to trouble her deeply.

155

She bent forward. 'You mustn't worry about it any more now,' she said soothingly. 'Just try to rest and get better.'

When Gail picked Rick up from Peter's house, on the outskirts of Lullford, he seemed quite happy at the prospect of spending the rest of the weekend at her new flat, but on the drive back to Hemmingbury Road he was unusually quiet. Gail realized that he must still be upset and worried about Aunt Lottie. It was understandable; after all, she had brought him up. It must have been very frightening for him, seeing her collapse like that.

'Don't worry about Aunt Lottie, Rick,' she said gently.

He looked at her. 'She won't – won't *die*, will she, Gail?'

'Of course she won't. She's got something called diabetes, but now that it's been diagnosed she'll be fine. Thousands of people have it and live perfectly normal lives.'

'Are you sure?'

'I'm certain. In fact once she's got used to the proper medicine and diet she'll be feeling better than she has for a very long time.'

'Does that mean she won't get so tired and – and cross?'

'She certainly won't.'

He glanced at her sideways. 'So does that

156

mean I won't have to go away to school?'

Gail looked at the hopeful brown eyes and her heart went out to the boy. 'Well – I wouldn't like to say that,' she told him. 'You'll have to wait and see what happens.'

Moments after they arrived back at the flat Kev tapped on the door.

'I wondered if everything was all right,' he said when Gail opened it. 'And if there was anything I could do.'

'Thanks, but there's nothing,' Gail said. 'Mrs Blake is in hospital. She has diabetes. I can't locate either Martin or Frances and Martin's sister is away for the weekend, so I've brought Patrick here with me for the weekend.'

'I see.' Kev grinned at the boy. 'Rick and I have met before, haven't we, Rick? Tell you what, why don't you and I take Gail swimming tomorrow?'

Rick looked doubtfully at Gail. 'Well – I'd like that, but…'

'I don't swim,' Gail put in. 'But it needn't stop you two. The only thing is, I haven't the supplies to make a picnic.'

'No problem. I have everything we'll need,' Kev said with a smile. 'I suggest we get together at nine o'clock tomorrow morning at my place.'

Rick brightened visibly at the suggestion and for that reason Gail was happy to accept Kev's invitation. She'd been wondering how to entertain the boy tomorrow. It was later, while they were eating supper, that Rick said suddenly, 'I've just remembered. I haven't got my pyjamas or toothbrush.'

'I always keep a new toothbrush by me,' Gail said. 'And you can manage without pyjamas for one night.'

'But I'll need my swimming trucks for tomorrow,' he insisted. 'Can't manage without *them*, can I?'

Gail sighed. She felt exhausted both physically and emotionally, and the thought of driving back to Hannerford House for a second time that evening was dismaying. However, there seemed nothing else for it. The boy couldn't go swimming without his trunks and she had promised. 'All right,' she said. 'Help me wash up these things then we'll drive over and get them.'

It was almost dark by the time they arrived at Hannerford House and the first thing Gail saw as they came in sight of the house was Martin's dark blue Porsche parked by the front door. Her heart quickened. Why was he here? He must have been puzzled, wondering where everyone was. The front door was ajar and Rick ran in ahead of her.

'Run up to your room and get what you need,' she told him. 'I'll go and tell Martin about Aunt Lottie.'

Standing at the foot of the stairs she heard

voices coming from the drawing-room. Martin had obviously brought someone back with him. Suddenly there was a loud pop and Frances's voice exclaimed with a laugh, *'Oh!* I never get used to champagne corks.'

'It was a bit of luck finding this in Father's cellar.' It was Martin's voice this time. 'Here you are. Here's to us – and the future!'

'To us – and to the future – yours and mine.'

As the glasses clinked Gail walked purposefully towards the door, anxious that they should know they were not alone. As she walked into the room she saw Martin and Frances standing by the fireplace, their champagne glasses poised halfway to their lips as their startled eyes turned towards her.

'Gail!' Frances found her voice first. 'What is it? Is anything wrong?'

'I'm afraid there is. I'm sorry to interrupt your – celebration,' she said, her cheeks pink. 'I did try to contact you both. Your aunt collapsed earlier this evening. She's in hospital.'

Martin put down his glass. 'Collapsed, you say? Do they know what's wrong?'

'It was hyperglycaemia.'

Martin looked stunned. 'But – she isn't diabetic.'

'I'm afraid she is,' Gail told him shortly.

'Luckily Rick telephoned me and I got here before she became too deeply unconscious. I couldn't locate you, so I sent for Peter. She's going to be all right, but...' She looked at Frances. 'She expressed an urgent wish to speak to you, Frances.'

The champagne forgotten, they both hurried towards the door. Martin stopped halfway. 'What about Rick? Is he all right?'

'He's fine. He was a very brave boy. If he hadn't rung me when he did...' She left the sentence unfinished. 'Don't worry about him. He can stay with me for the rest of the weekend.'

'Thanks, but that won't be necessary. I'll take charge of Rick now,' Martin said. 'If only we'd known about this earlier.'

'I did try to contact you,' Gail told him. 'I left messages for both of you on your machines, but–'

Martin broke in, 'Frances and I had some business to attend to.'

But Gail had heard the excitement in both their voices while she stood in the hall. She could imagine what kind of business it was.

'Martin! Aunt Lottie is in hospital!' Rick came clattering downstairs, a sports bag bulging with hastily packed clothing under his arm. 'I'm going to sleep at Gail's new flat.'

'I know about Aunt Lottie. Don't worry, Rick, she'll be fine. And now that I'm here

160

you can come home with me,' Martin said.

Rick's face fell. 'Oh! Do I *have* to? I was going to the beach for the day tomorrow with Gail and Kev – Mr Donaghue.'

'Oh! I *see!*' Martin looked at Gail, his eyebrows raised enquiringly. 'In that case, isn't Rick going to be in the way?'

It was loaded question and for a moment they stared at each other coldly. Gail felt the indignant colour rise in her cheeks as she said crisply, 'Of course he won't.' She dropped an arm across Rick's shoulders. 'I'm sure that the three of us will have a very pleasant day together. In any case, you and Frances must have a lot to attend to.'

Frances was looking from one to the other, her face troubled.

'Gail – perhaps you and Martin should have a private talk.'

'I doubt whether I have anything to say that would interest Gail,' Martin interrupted starkly.

'I'd better be getting Rick home to bed now,' Gail said quickly, steering the boy past Frances without meeting her eyes. 'There'll be plenty of time for talking later – if there's anything to say.'

When Gail woke next morning, sunlight flooded the room. It was going to be a perfect summer day. Just for a moment she wondered where she was. Then she remembered, she was in the new flat, and Rick was asleep in a makeshift bed she'd made up for him on her settee in the next room. Today they were going to the beach for the day with Kev. For a moment she wondered why she had wakened with such a heavy heart, then the reason surged back into her mind, shutting out the sunlight like a dark cloud. Martin and Frances were finally officially engaged. She herself had spoiled their celebration last night when she had walked in unexpectedly, like an avenging angel, to give them the news about Aunt Lottie. Frances's words echoed mockingly, 'Gail – perhaps you and Martin should have a private talk.' At least she had avoided that. It was embarrassing enough that Frances had guessed her feelings for Martin. She could at least save herself the humiliation of listening to Martin attempting to let her down lightly. That she couldn't have borne.

Last night she had fallen asleep with her mind in turmoil, but a night's sleep seemed to have clarified her thoughts and made up her mind. She would hand in her notice tomorrow morning. End all the uncertainty and heartache once and for all.

'Gail. What time is it?' Rick stood in the open doorway rubbing his eyes.

She peered at her alarm-clock, swallowing back the threatened tears. 'Half-past seven. I suppose we'd better get up and have some breakfast.' She threw back the duvet and reached for her dressing-gown, thankful for Rick's presence. But for him – and Kev, she might have spent the day brooding. At least they would give her no opportunity for that.

The day was fine and warm and Rick and Kev obviously enjoyed their day at the beach. Gail did her best to hide her despondency, but with Kev spending most of the time in the water with a delighted Rick she had plenty of time for thinking.

Later, back at the flat, she made supper for the three of them while Kev slipped out to buy a bottle of wine and Coke for Rick, to go with it.

Rick watched her pensively while she cooked. 'Would you like to marry Kev, Gail?' he asked suddenly.

She looked round at him in surprise. 'That's a funny thing to say. What makes you ask?'

The boy shrugged. 'Dunno. But if you do, can I come and live with you? I wouldn't have to go away to school then, would I?'

Gail ruffled his hair affectionately. Poor Rick. The dread of that school was constantly on his mind. 'It's a very good school. You'll make lots of new friends,' she told him. 'You'll see.'

Rick pulled a face. 'Want to bet?' he said gloomily.

For his sake she made a special effort and

163

they were toasting one another merrily, their meal almost finished, when there was a knock at the door. Gail went to answer it and found Martin standing on the threshold.

'I thought I'd come and collect Rick.' He stepped inside as she held the door open. 'And I wanted to talk–' He stopped, looking past her at the supper table where Rick and Kev still sat. 'Oh! I'm sorry if I'm interrupting,' he said stiffly.

'I was going to drive Rick over after supper,' Gail said, her cheeks pink.

'No doubt, but I can save you the trouble.' His tone was crisp as he beckoned to his young brother. 'Get your things, Rick. It's time to go.'

Kev picked up the wine bottle. 'Come and have a glass of wine with us, Martin,' he invited, but Martin remained where he was by the door, his mouth set in a grim line.

'No, thank you. Rick has to go to school tomorrow. It's time he was in bed.'

'How is Mrs Blake?' Gail asked.

'She's getting better by the minute.' He looked at her. 'I didn't thank you yesterday – for all you did.'

'I only sent for Peter – and the ambulance.'

'No, you did much more than that. You made the correct diagnosis and acted promptly,' he said.

'It wasn't all that difficult. I'd had my suspicions that she might be a diabetic for some time,' she told him.

He stared at her. 'And you said *nothing?*'

'I tried to speak to her more than once – to get her to ask for medical advice. She wouldn't listen.'

'But why on earth didn't you mention it to me or to Frances?' He was glowering at her now, his face like thunder. 'Why didn't you make her see one of us?'

'It wasn't my place to *tell* her what to do, Martin. I was living in her house. I told you, I tried to advise – suggest. She just thought I was interfering.'

'To begin with, you were living in *my* house, Gail, not Aunt Lottie's,' he said angrily. 'And as a nurse it was your duty to report your suspicions to me, not keep them yourself.'

'Was it my duty to tell you your job?' she challenged. 'To point out to you what was there in front of your eyes. She's your aunt. Where was *your* duty as a doctor, Martin?'

Rick had returned now with his packed bag. Martin turned and opened the door. 'Come along now, Rick. We're going.'

The boy glanced apologetically at Gail as he passed in front of his brother. 'Thank you for having me, Gail,' he said. 'I had a really fantastic day with you and Kev.'

Martin turned to Gail. 'Thank you for

165

looking after him,' he said unsmilingly. 'I'll see you at the surgery in the morning. Goodnight.'

As Gail closed the door behind them Kev blew out his breath in a long low whistle. 'Phew! Of all the ungrateful...' He shook his head at her. 'I don't know what's come over Martin Hannerford. He's just not the same guy I met when I first came here. I thought once that he and I were mates, but lately – I just don't know. What the hell got into him?'

Gail sank into the chair opposite him, her shoulders drooping and her throat tight. 'I'm no wiser than you are, Kev. I wish I were. You're right. In Northbridge Martin was a totally different person – carefree, popular, fun to be with.' She lifted her shoulders helplessly. 'But ... but now...' on the last word her voice threatened to wobble and she rose hurriedly to her feet and began to clear the table.

As she bent her head over the stacked dishes Kev watched her thoughtfully, noting her trembling hands as she clattered the dishes on to the tray. Suddenly the truth dawned on him. So *that* was it? It was Martin she was in love with. Poor kid! He stood up and took the tray gently from her.

'Leave that. Come and sit down. Tell Uncle Kev all about it.'

Gail allowed herself to be led to an armchair. 'There isn't anything to tell, Kev,' she

166

said. 'The Martin I used to know doesn't exist any more.'

'That isn't true,' he told her. 'Something must have happened to make him change. He's still the same underneath. Maybe it's all the new responsibilities he's suddenly coping with.' He crouched beside her, looking into her eyes. 'You love him, don't you?' he asked quietly.

She shook her head firmly. 'No! Not any more.'

'Are you sure?'

She took a deep breath in an effort to convince herself that she believed what she was saying. 'I'm sure. In fact I shall be handing in my notice first thing tomorrow morning.'

Kev looked at her for a long moment, then he said, 'I've known something was bugging you all day. Look, as soon as the rig is operational Mellex will be moving me on to another job. How about applying for a job with the company? We might even find ourselves working together.'

'It – sounds like a great idea.' Gail tried to sound enthusiastic, but her heart was sinking. Kev was hoping for too much, just as she once had. Heaven forbid that she should hurt him as she had been hurt.

But Kev was watching her face with a wry smile. 'It's no use, is it, love? You're trying hard but it isn't working. You still love the guy, so why fool yourself.'

His kind words were too much and she gave in to the tears that had threatened. 'Oh, Kev, I've tried, I really have. What am I going to do?'

He held her gently as she leaned against him. 'You've already made the decision to move away. That seems a wise idea for starters,' he said. 'After that – well, there's no short cut. Only time'll do it, I'm afraid.'

She lifted her head to look at him. 'You sound as though you're speaking from experience.'

He nodded, his expression rueful. 'It's true that I always wanted to see the world, but there was more than one reason for me leaving Aussie. Believe me, love, I do know how you feel. I crossed the world to escape from my unhappiness, but it made no difference. Not seeing the person helps but it's time, not distance, in the end!'

Gail arrived at the surgery early the following morning. As she let herself into the building all was quiet. She had noticed that Martin's car wasn't in its usual place in the car park, so she assumed that he had spent the night at Hannerford House. Before she had taken off her coat she went into Martin's room and laid the envelope containing her resignation on his desk.

Fay had arrived when she went back to the

office. She looked pale and there were lines of strain around her eyes. Gail remembered suddenly that her appointment with the consultant was this afternoon.

'I know it's easy to say, but try not to worry, Fay.' She laid a hand on the other girl's arm.

Fay turned dark-ringed eyes to her. 'I hardly slept at all last night.'

'Have you told your husband yet? Is he going to the hospital with you?'

Fay shook her head. 'Where's the sense in worrying him too?'

'I thought that was what husbands were for,' Gail said. 'To help and support you at times like this.'

'He's had a lot of worry at work lately,' Fay said. 'He's had redundancy hanging over his head for weeks now. I can't add to his anxiety, can I? Wives aren't there for that.'

'Well, if you want me to go with you just say,' Gail told her. 'The afternoon calls will just have to go on to the machine for once.'

But Fay shook her head. 'This is something I have to cope with myself, but thank you all the same.'

Gail went to her room and changed into her uniform. She had just sat down at her desk to sort through the pile of cards Fay had placed there ready for morning surgery when the door opened and Martin strode in, his face dark with anger.

'What does this mean?' He tossed her letter of resignation on to the desk in front of her.

'It's my notice.'

'But why? Why do you want to leave?'

'It isn't working, Martin. I – we both made a mistake. I should never have come here.'

'I see. I'm sorry you feel like that. But I suspect that it isn't the only reason!'

'It isn't! Ever since I first arrived I've been at cross purposes with everyone. I've taken the blame for everything – from delaying Fay's treatment to – to *alienating your affections!* Being blamed for not warning you that your aunt was ill was just the last straw!'

He sighed wearily. 'I wasn't blaming you, Gail. I know that you saved Aunt Lottie's life and I'll always be grateful. I was a bit overwrought last night. Surely you aren't leaving just for *that?*'

Just for that! Gail rose from her chair, almost dizzy with anger. It was time she said what was really in her mind and there would never be a better opportunity than this. Adrenalin pumping through her veins, she faced him, her eyes bright and her cheeks pink.

'No! If you must know, Martin, there's a lot more to it than that. In Northbridge you made me believe that I was – important to you. Perhaps I was naïve, but I honestly thought that when you offered me this job, you – well, you wanted *me* rather than just someone to fill a vacancy. I didn't know the truth about your situation until I arrived here. Even then you managed to string me along with your talk of trust and – and *complications*. You've made a fool of me, Martin. And perhaps I have only myself to blame for that. But now I've had enough and I want to leave.'

He was staring at her. 'You're talking in riddles, Gail. What truth? Who's been talking to you?'

'I heard you and Frances toasting each other in champagne on Saturday evening. I've seen the ring that she wears secretly around her neck. I've no idea what all the secrecy is about, but I've always hated anything devious.' She was well into her stride now. He took a step towards her, frowning, but she held out her hands to ward him off. 'No! Don't come near me. I won't pretend that it didn't hurt at first. But now I've seen you for what you are and I couldn't care less!' She walked back round her desk and faced him across it. 'I'd be grateful if you'd look for another nurse immediately. I'll work out my notice, of course, but I can't tell you what a relief it will be to get away from here. Being here – working in Lullford – makes Northbridge seem like Utopia!'

He stood there for a moment, his expression dark with fury. 'Right! Now you can

171

listen to what *I* have to say. You've changed too, Gail. You say I made you believe you were important to me. Did you really think so little of me that you also believed I'd lead you on just to get you into this job? What you're suggesting is preposterous! If you really believe it then maybe you're right to leave!'

'I intend to! Don't bother, Martin. I don't want to stay. I don't want to hear your explanations either – even if you offered any, which you haven't!'

'I fully intended to put everything straight between us last night,' he told her. 'But when I arrived I found Donaghue with you.'

Her head snapped up to look at him, her eyes blazing. 'Kev has been a good friend. And I've never needed someone to talk to more than I have these last few weeks.'

His eyes darkened, blazing back at her. 'Because of *me?* I see! I'm sorry to have caused you so much *trauma* that you had to turn to him!'

She shrugged, feigning nonchalance. 'There's no point in discussing it, Martin. It's over.'

'Well, I'm glad you'll at least have someone to help you pick up the pieces!'

'So am I!'

He picked up her letter of resignation from the desk where he had dropped it. 'So – I'm to take this as your last word, am I?'

'*Certainly.* There's no point in discussing it further. As far as I'm concerned there's nothing more to be said. Besides, the patients must be waiting.' In a dismissive gesture she began to sort through the cards on her desk. A moment later she heard the door slam behind him. The names on the cards swam illegibly before her tear-filled eyes. It was done. All her boats were burned. All that remained was for the wind to scatter the ashes. As Kev had said: time, not distance was the only healer. And she had the feeling she was going to need an awful lot of it.

CHAPTER NINE

When Gail arrived for evening surgery Fay was already there. It was clear at once from her smiling face that her visit to the consultant had not been as terrible as she'd feared.

'How did it go, Fay?' Gail asked as she took off her coat.

'The consultant was encouraging and very kind,' Fay told her. 'Though he was concerned that I'd left it so long. For that reason he wants me to go into hospital for a couple of days next week and have the lump surgically removed.'

'Oh, dear. I'm sorry to hear that,' Gail said.

'Oh, don't be.' Fay sounded confident. 'He assures me that it's a very simple operation and only a precautionary measure. That way they can do a proper biopsy so as to be absolutely sure.' She smiled. 'Oh, and I've told Bob, by the way.'

'Well, I'm glad about that. How did he take it?'

'He was worried at first. And cross that I'd kept it to myself all these months. But I feel so much better for his support. And that I've made a positive move. I can't wait now to get it over with.' She looked at Gail thoughtfully. 'Talking of moves, I rang Dr Grant when I got home, to tell her my news, and she told me you're leaving!'

'Yes. It won't affect your op though. I have a month's notice to work out.'

'It's not that. I'm just sorry you're going, Gail,' Fay said with genuine regret. 'I think we've all worked well together.'

'Well – some of us have.'

There was a pause, then Fay said, 'Yes, well I won't ask questions. I just thought you'd like to know my news.'

Gail worked through the evening surgery under a cloud. The next four weeks were going to be difficult, to say the least. Already a shocked Frances had tried to talk her out of leaving. Clearly, Martin had warned her not to get into a discussion about it, and when she had seen that Gail was determined she had dropped the subject and they had lapsed into an uneasy silence.

Then there had been Peter. But he had simply mentioned it briefly, giving her a sympathetic smile. After their conversation that evening down by the harbour he understood her motives and was too considerate to ask embarrassing questions.

It was the following evening that Gail answered the telephone to find a shocked Celia on the other end of the line. 'Gail!

Martin has been over to dinner and he's told us that you're leaving!'

'That's right.' Gail sighed. There seemed no end to it. She would be glad when everyone knew.

'But you will still be here for my wedding, won't you?'

'Well – yes. I'll still be here. But under the circumstances–'

'*What* circumstances? Of course you must still come,' Celia's voice was insistent. 'You helped me a lot when James and I had that silly quarrel. Look, I hope I've done the right thing, but I've sent an invitation to Kev Donaghue. I know you and he are friends, and I thought you could come together.'

'Oh! Yes, I'm sure he'd love to come. How is Mrs Blake?' Gail asked, changing the subject.

'She's getting along fine. She'll be home in a couple of days, in plenty of time for the wedding. We're all so grateful to you for what you did for her, Gail.'

'It was nothing.'

There was a pause, then Celia said, 'Gail, forgive me for asking, but it's fairly obvious that you and Martin have had some kind of row. Is there anything I can do to help?'

'No, Celia, there's nothing – thanks all the same.'

'Mmm. Well, if you do think of anything let me know. After all, one good turn deserves another. I'll see you at the wedding, then, not long to go now.'

'Of course – see you at the wedding.' Gail put down the phone feeling even more depressed than before. The sooner the month was out, and she could stop pretending, the better.

The following week, Fay went into hospital for her minor operation. Martin had arranged for a temporary receptionist to fill in. Mary Jennings had worked for the practice in Martin's father's time and had left to bring up her family, so she was familiar with the routine of the surgery.

Fay's small operation was straightforward and she was out of hospital two days later. She came in at the end of the week to have her stitches removed, looking, and obviously feeling, much better. As Gail gently snipped and removed the sutures Frances looked on.

'He's obviously a considerate surgeon,' she observed. 'Those are cosmetic sutures like the ones used in plastic surgery. You'll barely see the scar once it heals.'

Fay smiled. 'I know. And he says he's almost certain that everything is all right,' she told them. 'But just to be sure we have to wait for the biopsy result to confirm it. I shall know when I go back for my post op check.' She looked at Frances. 'If only I'd known how it would be before. If we could get the message across to other women that it's really important to get help and advice at an early stage,' she said. 'If I'd gone sooner I might even have been saved the two days in hospital.'

Frances nodded thoughtfully. 'You're right. A real person, especially someone everyone knows, standing up and telling her own personal experience would be even better than a video. Would you be willing to do that for us, Fay?'

'Yes, I would. I'm not very good at public speaking but I'd do my best. I'd like to think I could put what I went through to some positive use.'

Frances's eyes were sparkling. 'We could have some informal lectures – maybe even get a consultant along. What do you think?' She turned to Gail, then her enthusiastic smiled faded. 'Oh – I was forgetting, you won't be here, will you?'

Gail's heart sank. Once again she had the dreaded feeling of not belonging anywhere. She would have loved to have been part of the health re-education programme for women that Frances was planning. It was so vitally important. But now it was just another fading dream. 'No,' she said quietly as she turned away. 'No, I won't be here.'

It was four days before Celia's wedding that Gail had a surprise visitor one evening.

178

Arriving home at the flat, she found Lottie Blake waiting outside in her car.

'Mrs Blake! Come in and have some tea. Are you sure you should be out?'

'I'm fine now,' Lottie assured her. 'Never better – as long as I'm sensible with my diet and remember my insulin I'm promised a full and normal life.' She walked up the stairs with Gail. 'At least, as full and normal as any woman of my age can expect.'

Gail observed Lottie as she made the tea. The older woman did indeed look much better than she had ever seen her. She seemed more relaxed and the fact that she had put on a little weight made her look ten years younger. As Gail put the tray down on the coffee-table, Lottie said, 'I may as well come to the point: I hear that you're leaving us.'

'Yes.' Gail sighed. She would have preferred not to discuss it yet again.

'I'm sorry. I really came this evening for two reasons. First to thank you for all that you did and, second...' Lottie looked uneasy '...second, to ask you to keep to yourself what I told you at the hospital that evening.'

'About Frances being your daughter, you mean?'

'Yes.' Lottie sighed. 'I'm afraid I was a little over-emotional that evening. I've discovered since that there's very little chance of her inheriting my diabetes, so I feel that, all things considered, it's better to let things stay as they are.'

'So you don't want her to know you're her mother for – other reasons?'

Lottie looked wistful. 'It's her I'm thinking of. What young woman would want to hear that her father had served a jail sentence for bigamy and embezzlement?'

'But to know that *you* are her mother would surely make up for that,' Gail said.

Lottie smiled.' It's sweet of you to say so, dear. But I've thought it over and I think I'd rather not risk spoiling the happy relationship we already have, especially as she's soon to be married.' Impervious to Gail's small gasp, she looked at her watch and rose from the chair. 'Well, I must be going. It'll soon be time for my injection. Thank you for the tea, and I'm glad we're to see you at the wedding, in spite of everything.'

Gail rose with her and as they walked to the door together she said, 'Mrs Blake, one thing still puzzles me. You said something else that night at the hospital, something about talking your brother into doing something that you now regretted.'

Lottie paused. 'Ah, yes. I thought I'd explained that. I think I was a little confused that evening. It was just before John died. I talked him into making a codicil to his will, stipulating that unless Martin had married Frances within a year of his death Hannerford House and the practice would pass to Frances alone.' She sighed. 'I've had many a bad night's sleep agonising about it since. It was a dreadful thing to do – almost like playing God. But I felt so ill at the time, and I was anxious about Frances and her future. A man is so much more able to look after himself, don't you think?' She smiled and drew a relieved sigh. 'But there, as it happens I needn't have worried, need I? It's all worked out for the best.' She laid a hand on Gail's arm. 'My only regret now is that you didn't feel your place was here with us after all. We shall all miss you, dear.'

Gail walked downstairs to the car with Lottie and stared thoughtfully after it as she drove away. So *that* was it! Martin was marrying his cousin so that he could inherit his father's estate? No wonder Lottie thought everything was working out for the best. Her daughter was to marry Martin, just as she had always planned. And Gail – the only person who knew her secret – would soon be hundreds of miles away!

As she walked slowly back up the stairs she tried to convince herself that if Martin was the kind of man who would marry for money, then she was certainly well rid of him! Curiously, it didn't make her feel any better.

Kev often spent days at a time working on

the rig, especially now that it was nearing completion and Gail had already worked almost two weeks of her notice before she saw him again. He called in to show her the wedding invitation he'd found waiting on his doormat when he returned to the flat the following weekend. It was then that she broke the news that she was leaving.

'So you really went ahead and did it?' he said when she told him her news. 'How did Martin take it?'

She shrugged. 'We had a blazing row. I told him a few home truths – probably said more than I should. It made me feel better – at the time.' She avoided his searching eyes. 'We haven't spoken since and Frances is distinctly cool with me too. I'll be glad now when it's time to pack up and leave. I wouldn't be going to the wedding except that I promised Celia.'

'Are you having regrets, Gail? Because if you want to do something to put things right you shouldn't let your pride stand in the way. Sometimes we don't get a second chance, you know.'

Something about his tone made her look at him. He looked tired and grubby, but there was something else about him, a look in his eyes she couldn't quite read. 'Is everything all right, Kev?' she asked.

'I'm pretty crooked,' he admitted. 'We've had a few kinks in the system this week out there on the rig. You know, awkward little hitches that make life difficult. I think we have them all licked now, though.' He grinned. 'I'm fine really. At least, I will be when I've had a hot bath and a good feed.'

'Eat with me,' she said impulsively. 'My week has been pretty gruesome too. I could do with some friendly company. And we can decide what to get Celia and James for a wedding present.'

She already had a beef casserole in the oven and there was plenty for two. By the time Kev reappeared she was dishing it up.

He sniffed appreciatively. 'Smells good.'

'It should. I added some red wine,' she told him, pointing to the bottle she had opened. 'Help yourself to a glass.'

Over the meal she discovered the reason for his pensive mood earlier. He told her that among the mail waiting for him on his return was a letter from home.

'There was some rather unsettling news in it.' He tried to sound casual as he helped himself to more casserole, but Gail sensed that he needed to talk about it.

'What was that?' she asked.

'The girl I used to be keen on just got a divorce.' He said. 'She and I grew up together. We were pretty close at one time, then I went away to college and came home to find her engaged to a mate of mine.'

'And she married him?' Gail asked.

He nodded. 'Just about broke me up at the time, though I never let on to anyone.'

'What was she like, Kev?' Gail asked gently.

He looked at her with a wistful smile. 'Jill? She's a lot like you, Gail, which is why I took to you from the first minute we met.'

'I see. So now that the marriage is over, how do you feel, Kev?'

'I don't know.' He studied his plate for a moment. 'I suppose I should be sorry. Maybe I should be telling myself I was well out of it. On the other hand I can't help wondering if the marriage failed because she realised she'd married the wrong guy.' He looked at her. 'I'm pretty mixed up, I guess – except that at the back of my mind there's this persistent little voice that keeps telling me I might be back in there with another chance. If only I knew how *she* felt. That's what's so unsettling. Being so far away isn't easy.'

'You could always write to her.'

'I guess I could at that. She could always write back and tell me to get lost!'

'And if she didn't – if she said she wanted to see you again?'

He sighed. 'Yeah – well, I hardly dare think about that possibility.'

'But it's something you *should* think through before you write, isn't it?' She looked searchingly at him. 'Do you still love her – enough to pack up your job here – to go back and try again?'

Kev's worried expression suddenly dissolved into the familiar grin. *'Can a duck swim?'* He laughed and then suddenly remembered something. Diving into the pocket of his jacket, he brought out an envelope. 'Oh, I almost forgot. I sent for an application form for you. I guess you're probably going to need it, now!' He passed it across the table to her. 'What about you anyway?' he asked. 'We've been talking on and on about me and you've been having a miserable time. This row you had with Martin – any chance of you making it up?'

Gail shook her head. 'None at all. Anyway, I heard a couple of days ago that he's definitely marrying Dr Frances Grant.'

He smiled sympathetically. 'So that's that, then? I'm really sorry, kid. But we'll have a ball at this wedding, eh? Let's show 'em we don't give a damn. I hope you've got something knock-out to wear.'

'I'm working on it,' she said without much enthusiasm.

'Great! Going out in a blaze of glory, eh?'

In fact, Gail had done nothing at all about her outfit for Celia's wedding, but Kev's words made her realise that she owed it to herself to put on a good front. *Going out in a blaze of glory* was hardly how she saw it, but,

185

all the same, her pride refused to let her heartbreak show. So on the Thursday afternoon before the wedding Fay agreed to come in, and man Reception, while she went shopping.

She found nothing she liked in the first two shops she tried, but in the third she saw an outfit that really caught her eye. The price ticket almost took her breath away and she turned away. But although she looked at other dresses none of them quite came up to the first one. She took it off the rail and held it against herself in front of the mirror, wondering whether she could carry it off. It was bolder and more sophisticated than anything she had worn before, a two-piece in printed silk with a striking pattern of black orchids on a white background. But the moment she tried it on it seemed to lift her spirits and give her confidence. The skirt was finely pleated and swirled fluidly around her legs as she moved. The well cut top had a cross-over neckline and tiny nipped-in waist. To team with it, Gail bought black patent sandals and a white straw hat with a black silk rose nestling under the wide brim against her blonde hair.

A visit to the hairdresser was her next priority. Fay had recommended Paolo, a young Italian stylist who had recently opened a salon in Lullford High Street.

Throwing caution to the winds, she allowed him to restyle her hair as he pleased and she emerged an hour later with a completely new look. Paolo had brought her hair forward, cutting it in a feathery fringe that enhanced the size and shape of her eyes. He had also taken off some of the length so that the delicate bone-structure of her face was revealed. The new bouncy style seem to restore her confidence and as she drove home afterwards she found that for the first time she was almost looking forward to the wedding.

As she put her key into the lock she heard the telephone ringing. Opening the door, she tossed her parcels into a chair and picked up the receiver.

'Hello, Gail Ingram here.'

'Gail! Oh, good. I was just about to hang up,' Celia's voice said at the other end. 'I wanted to invite you to a little get together tomorrow evening. Just a few of my friends, here at home. James will be having his stag night, so I thought I should have a party too. You will come, won't you?'

'Thank you, Celia. I'd like that.'

'Super. About eight. Aunt Lottie is laying on a little supper, so don't eat first.'

Gail replaced the receiver and stood looking down at it thoughtfully. It would have been churlish to have refused Celia's invitation, but it would feel odd, going to

Hannerford House again. Frances would obviously be there. The coolness between them was just possible to cope with when they were working together, but she wasn't sure how easy they would be with each other in a social situation. Frances's own wedding plans would obviously come up for discussion during the evening, too. It promised to be an uncomfortable occasion all round.

Gail was ten minutes late arriving at Hannerford House the following evening. A starry-eyed Celia opened the door to her, greeting her warmly. 'Gail. I'm glad you could come. Everyone's here. We're all in the drawing-room, do come in and have a glass of wine.'

'This is from Kev and me,' Gail handed over the gift-wrapped wedding present she had chosen on behalf of Kev and herself the previous afternoon.

'Oh, thank you. I can't wait to see what it is!' Celia was like a little girl as she unwrapped the box in the dining-room where all her other gifts were displayed. When she saw the Mayling fruit bowl inside, with its pattern of richly coloured pansies, she exclaimed with delight. 'Oh – it's *lovely*, Gail!'

'I saw it in an antique shop and I knew at once you'd like it,' Gail told her. 'Mayling is getting quite rare and collectable.'

'I shall cherish it!' Celia held the bowl up to the light, admiring its lustrous pearly glaze. 'Everyone is going to covet this.' She put it with the other presents and hugged Gail. 'Thanks again and thank Kev for me too, will you? Now come and say hello to the others. You haven't met many of them before, but Frances is here.'

At first glance, the drawing-room seemed full of strangers as Gail stood in the doorway, then Lottie Blake came forward and took her hands, drawing her into the room. 'Listen, everyone,' she said, her voice rising above the chatter. 'This is Nurse Gail Ingram. But for her I wouldn't be here to celebrate Celia's wedding. She saved my life.'

There was a hush as all eyes turned towards her and Gail froze with embarrassment. Then Frances rose and came to her rescue. 'Come and be introduced,' she said. 'And have a glass of wine and one of Aunt Lottie's cheese straws. She's famous for them.'

When the introductions were over, and the attention was off Gail once more, she turned to Frances with relief. 'Thanks for helping me out. That was awful!'

'Aunt Lottie meant well.' Frances smiled. 'Anyway, what she said was true. She'll never forget what you did.' She poured a glass of wine and handed it to Gail. 'Shall we change the subject? Did you have any

189

luck with your wedding outfit yesterday?'

'Yes. I found what I wanted quite easily. You won't have had that problem as bridesmaid, of course.'

Frances pulled a face. 'Don't you believe it. I always feel that bridesmaiding is for the *very* young, don't you? I couldn't see myself in something pink and frilly. Celia agreed and we chose the dress together. I think it goes well with her own dress. We chose a medieval theme.' She glanced round. 'Would you like to come upstairs and see it? I don't think we'll be missed for five minutes.'

Upstairs in one of the spare bedrooms, Frances opened the wardrobe and took out her polythene-shrouded gown. As she removed the covering Gail gasped.

'Oh, Frances, it's beautiful!'

The dress was of Madonna-blue, in a heavy silk material. It was cut in a perfectly plain princess style, with long sleeves, pointed over the wrists and a low waistline flowing over the hips. The neckline was high, but straight across in front and dipping into a shallow V at the back. With Frances's auburn hair it would look stunning.

'You like it, then?' Frances said, looking pleased. 'I'm wearing my hair loose, caught back at one side with a white camellia, and I'll be carrying a sheaf of white flowers. Plain but effective, I think.'

'Oh, yes. You're going to look lovely.' Gail

paused. This seemed to be as good a time as any to put right the coolness that had hung between them over the past weeks. 'Frances – you do know I wish you well, don't you,' she said awkwardly. 'Both of you, I mean.'

'Both of us?' Frances looked puzzled. 'I don't understand. We haven't actually announced it yet – so how–'

'I've known for some time,' Gail said. 'I accidentally saw your ring one day at the surgery. And, when I came to tell you your aunt had been admitted to hospital, you and Martin were celebrating. Then Mrs Blake told me the other day about the codicil to Martin's father's will.' She moistened her dry lips. 'It's good that you and Martin love each other enough to make it work out.'

Frances was frowning. 'Wait a minute. Aunt Lottie told you that Martin and I–?'

'No, she didn't have to,' Gail said. 'I'd already guessed. She just said that it was a relief to her that everything was working out for the best.'

'And you assumed...' Frances sat down on the edge of the bed, staring at Gail. 'So *that's* what it's all been about? I think you and I have a few things to get straight, Gail. It's true that I'm engaged, but not to Martin.'

Gail's heart gave a lurch that almost took her breath away. *'Not* – then who?'

Frances sighed. 'His name is Graham

Dean. We were students together and we met again and fell in love on the obstetrics course I took a while ago. He asked me to marry him before the course was over, but I came home to find that Martin had discovered this horrendous codicil to his father's will in his desk here at home. Can you imagine how I felt? I had either to marry Martin, whom I've always thought of as a brother, or take his inheritance from him! Ken Mason, the solicitor, obviously hadn't known it existed, and we couldn't tell whether it was valid or not. To make matters worse, Ken had been ill and had gone away on an extended holiday, so we couldn't get in touch. You can imagine how worrying it all was.'

'But the day I saw you celebrating?'

'We'd been down to Cornwall for the day – to track Ken down and show him the codicil. It was my idea,' Frances said. 'I didn't want to keep my engagement a secret any longer and Martin wanted things out in the open, too. Ken examined the document and was able to tell us that it wasn't properly witnessed and therefore void. *That's* what we were celebrating!' Frances shook her head at Gail's stunned expression. 'Poor Gail. What a family we must have seemed to you – all secrets and conspiracies! And to think I've been so cross with you for hurting Martin.'

Hurting Martin! Gail looked away, biting her lip. 'He should have explained to me.

Why did he let me go on thinking the worst? Even when I gave my notice he didn't say anything about all this.'

'I kept telling him he should talk to you, but I think he was afraid of scaring you off. He kept hoping that things would work out. Then, when you said you didn't care any more...' Frances looked at her ruefully. 'Martin is a very proud man, like his father. And since he came home again he's had so much on his plate. His father left an awful lot of problems behind – things that even Celia and Aunt Lottie don't know about and, I suspect, some he's kept from me, too. He's shouldered all the worry himself – tried hard to shield us all – to sort it all out so that no one should suffer.'

Gail turned away. What Frances had told her made everything clear, but it was too late to help the ruined relationship between Martin and herself. Surely if he'd loved her – seen her as a future partner – he would have confided in her, drawn comfort from the sympathy and support she would gladly have given him. Now, though, after what she'd said to him on the day she'd given him her notice, things could never be the same between them. Since that day they'd communicated in monosyllables, and only when it was absolutely necessary. Suddenly she looked up and saw Frances watching her.

'Are you all right, Gail?'

'Of course. I'm fine.'

'You can always rescind your resignation, you know. I know Martin hasn't found another nurse yet.'

Gail had done nothing about the application forms Kev had given her either, though she didn't say so. 'It's no use, Frances,' she said. 'It could never be the same. Martin and I have both changed since we left Northbridge. And, anyway, I don't believe he was ever serious about me. All that was just a silly dream on my part. Hopefully, I've grown up now.' She forced a smile. 'We really should go downstairs, shouldn't we? Your aunt will be waiting to serve supper.'

'Yes.' But Frances didn't move. She was looking at Gail curiously. 'Gail – before we do, there's something I'd like to ask you: when Aunt Lottie was ill did she tell you anything about me?'

'No,' Gail lied, willing herself not to blush.

'For instance – that she is my natural mother?'

The colour that flooded Gail's cheeks spoke for her. 'She *did* tell you after all, then?'

Frances laughed at Gail's puzzled expression. 'I've known for years. Aunt Margaret told me before she died. I waited for a long time for Aunt Lottie to tell me herself, but she never did. I think we both know it's too late now. It was Aunt Margaret I always thought of as "Mother". When Aunt Lottie was ill you said she wanted to see me urgently and I thought she might be about to tell me then – that she'd treated you as a sort of "mother confessor".'

'She did,' Gail admitted. 'I think it was preying on her mind at the time. She was afraid you might inherit her complaint. But later, when she knew there was little risk of that, she decided to let things stay as they were.'

Frances smiled. 'She was right. It's better this way.' She burst into a sudden chuckle. 'Oh, dear! What a family, you must be thinking. Maybe you're happy to be opting out of it after all!'

Gail said nothing. How could she confess to Frances that, on the contrary, it was something she would regret for the rest of her life?

'Come on, let's go down.' Frances opened the door and they went out on to the landing. The sound of happy voices rose to meet them as they went down the stairs. Tomorrow the house would be alive with the bustle and excitement of Celia's wedding preparations.

And next week Gail would be saying goodbye to the Hannerford family – and to Martin – for ever.

CHAPTER TEN

The little church of St Swithin's stood within sight and sound of the sea. Stoutly built of grey stone and squat as a cottage loaf, it had withstood the strong winds from the English Channel for almost four hundred years. Gail and Kev arrived with time to spare and walked in at the lych-gate in the shade of centuries-old yew trees. In the porch they were greeted by Rick, resplendent in a new dark grey suit with a white carnation in the buttonhole, his unruly hair tamed and smartly slicked down. He informed them gravely that he was the chief usher and conducted them to a pew on the left-hand side of the aisle with the solemn dignity his role demanded.

Gail looked round the little church's interior with delight. The pew-ends were decorated with posies of cornflowers and lacy gypsophila, tied with white ribbon. Celia had chosen a theme of blue and white, and it seemed to Gail that blue and white flowers spilled and frothed from every window-sill. It was cool and tranquil inside the church and after the rush and excitement of preparation there was time to relax.

James and his best man were already seated in a front pew, and the organ played softly as the church gradually filled with friends and relatives.

Kev squeezed her hand. 'You look great, Gail,' he said. 'Do you feel OK?'

She nodded, smiling. 'I'm fine, Kev. I'm glad you're with me, though.'

A sudden rustling at the back of the church heralded the arrival of the bride and the guests rose as the organ struck up the first notes of the wedding march. As Celia passed on Martin's arm, Gail glanced round at her. She looked breathtaking. Her ivory dress was made of lustrous wild silk and cut, like Frances's, in a slim medieval style; it's long, tightly fitting sleeves were puffed at the shoulder and embroidered with tiny seed pearls. Her upswept dark hair was enclosed in a silver and pearl coronet from which flowed an elbow length veil. She seemed to glide on a cloud of fragrance from her all-white bouquet of roses and stephanotis. Gail glanced at Martin. He looked so handsome in his grey morning suit that she felt a sharp stab of pain in her heart. Kev sensed it and squeezed her hand again.

They passed, followed by Frances, looking stunning in her blue dress and for the first time Gail noticed a tall, fair-haired young man two pews in front of them, who turned and smiled up at Frances as she passed, with obvious love shining in his blue eyes. Gail swallowed hard. How was she to get through today? Suddenly it seemed to her that the whole world was in love all around her, with only herself as the interloper.

The simple, age-old ceremony brought a lump to Gail's throat and when the bride, groom and witnesses had gone to the vestry to sign the register she fumbled surreptitiously in her bag for a hanky. Without a word, Kev passed her his. She took it gratefully.

Outside in the sunny churchyard they waited while the photographs were taken, then, after the bride and groom had left in a colourful hail of confetti, Gail climbed into Kev's car with an audible sigh of relief.

'Glad it's over?' Kev asked as he started the engine.

'It was beautiful,' Gail said. 'They all looked wonderful and so happy.'

'They're a good-looking family, I grant you that. But it was more than the beauty of the occasion that was making you cry, wasn't it?'

When she didn't reply he turned and winked at her. 'Hey – shall I tell you something to make you laugh?'

Gail blinked hard. 'I think you'd better!'

'You know I was going to look up the records and try to find out a little about my

Dorset ancestors? Well, with the help of the local vicar, I went through the church records last night and guess what?'

'I can't imagine – tell me.'

He began to chuckle. 'Way back – oh, something like five or six generations, one of our females married a Hannerford! What do you think Martin would say if he knew that he and I were related?'

Gail looked at him for a moment, then the irony struck her too and she joined in his laughter. 'Will you tell him?'

'I might.' Kev's grin was mischievous. 'It's something to savour for a while first, though.'

The wedding reception was held at the Clifftop Hotel. A radiant Celia and smiling James were there to receive them, along with Aunt Lottie, Frances and, last in line, Martin. As she put her hand into his, Gail glanced up and his eyes held hers in a long, enigmatic look. She tried to read what she saw there, but found it impossible. Neither of them spoke and, aware of the next guest in the line waiting behind her, Gail moved on to take a glass of sherry from the proffered tray and mingle with the others.

The reception passed smoothly and happily; toasts were drunk, telegrams read, speeches made. Martin's, made in his role of 'brother of the bride', was witty and eloquent. The best man complimented Frances

199

on her elegance and beauty, then, last of all, came a surprise. Celia rose and, after thanking everyone concerned for the success of her wedding day, she announced the engagement of her bridesmaid, Frances Grant, to Dr Graham Dean. The couple stood, hand-in-hand, to receive the applause and congratulations of everyone present.

'Generous of Celia to step out of the limelight on her special day,' Kev remarked.

'Isn't it?' Gail looked at Frances's shining eyes and hated herself for jumping to all the wrong conclusions about the Hannerford family. She had been disastrously wrong about all of them – including Martin.

The bride and groom went off to change and the guests began to mingle. Kev left her to go and talk to someone on the other side of the room and Fay brought her husband over to meet Gail. They chatted for a while and Gail was pleased to notice how much younger and happier Fay was looking since she'd had the final result of her test from the hospital.

They had just moved away when she felt a light touch on her shoulder.

'Gail – may I sit down?'

She looked up to see Martin standing at her side and her cheeks flamed. 'Of course.' He took the chair the Kev had vacated.

'It's been a lovely wedding,' Gail said. 'Celia looks so happy.' She glanced up at him. 'Martin, I – owe you an apology.'

'And I owe you one, which is why I'm here. Let's take them as said, shall we?' They sat in silence for a moment or two then he said, 'I take it you've found another job?'

'I – I've got one in mind,' she said. She was finding it increasingly difficult, being so close to him, making small talk as though they were virtual strangers, when her heart ached with the longing to make everything right between them.

'That's good,' he said lightly. 'You'll be happier when it's all settled.'

Gail's heart sank lower as she glanced at him. They were talking like polite acquaintances. If a move were to be made, it clearly had to come from her. She swallowed hard. 'Frances tells me you've had some worrying problems with your father's estate,' she said. 'I – I wish I'd known that.'

He looked down at her. 'I take it we're talking about the codicil?' He gave her an ironic little smile. 'That's the least of my worries, Gail. As it happens it wouldn't have mattered much if the codicil *had* been valid.' She looked up at him with startled eyes and he explained, 'You see, in point of fact there's a very real danger of there being nothing to inherit.'

Her eyes widened with shock. 'Oh, *Martin!*'

'My father had invested heavily in the

stock market. When the crash came he mortgaged Hannerford House and tried more investments in a last desperate attempt to recoup his money. It seems he took some devastatingly bad advice and lost everything. He wanted so badly to leave us all well provided for, but all he actually left was a massive debt.'

Gail's mind was working fast. 'That was why you stopped the work going ahead to convert the house into flats?'

'Yes. I couldn't explain my reasons to poor Celia. I felt badly about that. About sending Rick away to school too, but what else could I do? I was going to have to tell them all sooner or later that the house they had called home for so many years must be sold.'

'And now?' Gail asked.

He shrugged. 'Things are looking slightly better. I've received a good offer from Mellex. If I agree to sell to them, they'll convert Hannerford House for use as onshore staff accommodation and offices. When the debts have been paid off I'll just be able to pay Rick's school fees and keep the practice afloat.'

'Need Rick really go away to school?' she asked.

'I'm afraid so.' He looked at her. 'But I've compromised by saying he can come home every weekend – just till we see how we manage.'

'Oh, Martin – your lovely family home,' she said. 'I'm so sorry.'

He shrugged. 'It can't be helped. What's done is done.'

'And Mrs Blake – where will she go?'

'Aunt Lottie has been one of my main worries. We owe her so much for what she's done for us over the years.' He smiled wryly. 'Even if she did almost cause havoc in our lives. What with that, and everything else, I completely failed to notice that she was ill. You can imagine how much worse I felt about the possibility of taking her home away from her once I knew.' For the first time he smiled. 'But, as it happens, that particular problem has solved itself. She told me a couple of days ago that once Rick goes away to school and there is nothing to keep her here, she wants to go and live with an old friend in Bournemouth.'

Silence fell between them. Gail wanted so much to ask him what *his* future plans were, but somehow she couldn't find the right words. Suddenly he stood up abruptly. 'Well, I'd better go and talk to someone else now. There are so many relatives who mustn't be left out. It would never do to offend anyone, would it?'

As he walked away his words echoed emptily in her mind. *Would never do to offend anyone.* Talking to her had been no more than a courtesy, then. He was right, she *would* feel better once she had some firm plans for her future. As soon as she got back to the flat tonight she would fill in the Mellex forms Kev had given her. She might even get the chance to travel – see the world. She tried hard to feel excited at the thought, but the heaviness in her heart refused to lift.

She was just about to go and look for Kev when she saw Lottie Blake coming towards her.

'My dear. I've been trying to get the chance of a word with you. You look so lovely. That black and white suits you perfectly.'

Gail smiled. 'Thank you, you look very nice yourself. I believe you've started to put a little weight on again.'

'I have, in spite of my sugar-free diet. And I'm feeling wonderful,' Lottie said. 'So much so, that I'm realising now just how ill I felt before.' She sat down in the chair Martin had vacated and laid a hand on Gail's arm. 'I saw you and Martin in earnest conversation just now. Have you made up your quarrel?'

'We're – friends again, yes,' Gail said guardedly.

'Does that mean...?'

'It doesn't mean I'm staying on,' Gail said, anticipating the older woman's question.

Lottie looked disappointed. 'Oh! I had hoped...' She bit her lip. 'Was it my meddling that ruined things between you and

Martin?' she asked. 'I've been wrong about so many things. I'm afraid my illness must have clouded my judgement. Now that I see how happy Frances is with Graham I wish I'd left well alone.' She looked at Gail, her brow furrowed with anxiety. 'Is there anything I can do to put things right for you? Forgive me, dear, but I can tell you still care very deeply for Martin.'

'There's nothing anyone can do,' Gail told her. 'Martin has plans for the future of the practice here at Lullford; plans which don't include me.' She could see that Lottie wasn't going to let the subject rest and she was grateful to see Kev crossing the room in their direction. 'I wanted a word with Kev Donaghue,' she said, getting to her feet. 'You will excuse me, Mrs Blake, won't you?'

As she grasped a slightly surprised Kev's hand she sighed with relief. 'Thanks for rescuing me.'

'I wasn't aware that you were in danger!' His eyebrows rose as he looked down at her. 'Mrs Blake doesn't look very vicious to me!'

'She was trying to persuade me to stay on; racking her brains to think of a way to patch things up between Martin and me.'

'Well? I can't see anything so terrible about that.'

'I have to face it, Kev. If there ever was anything between Martin and me, it's over now – over for keeps. And the sooner I get away from here, the better.'

He took one look at her face and said no more. It was clear that she wanted to close the subject.

Celia and James reappeared, dressed in their going-away clothes and everyone crowded out on to the drive of the hotel to wave them off. As they were coming back inside, a worried-looking receptionist stopped Gail.

'There's an urgent telephone call for a Mr Donaghue. Could you point him out to me, please?'

Kev was only feet away and he went off with the receptionist. A few minutes later he reappeared and made his way purposefully across the room to Martin. As she watched, Gail saw Martin's face grow serious and they glanced in her direction, then the two men were crossing the room towards her.

'There's been an explosion on the oil rig,' Martin told her quickly. 'Kev's just received an urgent call to go out. It seems there's some problem they can't locate – danger of more trouble. They need me as well. There are some casualties.'

'I'll come too,' Gail said at once.

Martin looked doubtful. 'I was going to ask you to explain to anyone who asked where we were. It's no place for a woman.'

'I'm not coming as a woman. I'm coming as a *nurse*,' Gail told him firmly. 'If there are casualties, then surely I can be of use.' She looked down at her clothes. 'Is there time to change?'

'I have to pick up my bag at the surgery on the way, but there's no time to lose,' Martin said.

'A chopper is on its way,' Kev told her. 'It'll pick us up at Hemmingbury, on that broad expanse of beach. There'll be overalls and hard hats on board so don't worry about your clothes. They're sending the lifeboat out to evacuate the rig, just to be on the safe side.'

Gail's heart was beating fast as they piled into Kev's car and headed for the surgery. Martin let himself in and reappeared moments later with his case and the Entonox equipment.

'I've alerted the hospital,' he told them. 'They'll have ambulances waiting on the beach and they're preparing to receive casualties.'

When they arrived at Hemmingbury, three miles along the coast, the helicopter was waiting, its blades still rotating. Gail's skirt flapped around her legs and she was hauled unceremoniously up into the craft, and seconds later she felt her stomach lurch as they took off swiftly, in a deafening rush of air and whirring rotor blades.

Kev handed out the overalls and hard hats and as they quickly pulled them on Gail reflected with a pang of regret that the arbitrary treatment was going to do nothing for her expensive new outfit. But that was the least of her anxieties. Although she tried not to show it, she was a little apprehensive about what lay ahead. She had worked in Accident and Emergency during her training, but had never dealt with anything like this. A glance at Kev's tense face told her that he was worried too. As chief engineer he held responsibility for many lives.

'Good thing there's only a skeleton crew on board,' he shouted above the roar of the engine. 'And that the weather's not too bad. Thank God it's still light too.'

'Any idea what caused the explosion?' Martin asked.

Kev shook his head. 'Could be one of several things. It's the one thing every engineer dreads. All I know is, it's my baby!' He peeped out of the window. 'Here we are. Hold on tight, Gail, we're coming in to land.'

Gail held her breath as the helicopter rapidly lost height to hover above the brightly painted circles on the drilling platform below. The pilot shouted, over his shoulder, 'Touching down! OK back there?'

'Fine!' Martin and Kev shouted together.

Martin touched Gail's hand. 'Are you all right?'

She nodded, swallowing hard. 'I think so.'

His expression softened as he looked at

her face and his fingers tightened round hers, giving them a reassuring squeeze.

The next moment there was a bump as they landed, then it was all action as the doors opened and they were helped out. In spite of the fact that it was a summer evening, the wind that hit them seemed to Gail like a force eight gale. It almost took her breath away as she was lifted out on to the helipad. Kev immediately disappeared from sight on his way to the seat of the trouble and the man who had lifted Gail out and who introduced himself as Ted Packer, the resident orderly, indicated that she and Martin were to follow him. 'We've put the casualties in the mess. Didn't like to move them too far,' he said.

'How many?' Martin asked.

'Four.' The man opened the door. 'Two engineers; the other two were hurt fighting the fire.'

Gail's anxiety was quickly forgotten when she saw the casualties. Two of them had burns more severe than she had ever seen before and were clearly suffering from severe pain and shock. Martin made a brief examination and turned to her. 'All we can hope to do is ease the pain and administer first aid,' he said quietly. 'These two are going to need immediate surgery.'

The other two men had lesser burns, but one of them had a badly fractured wrist and a head wound. It was clear that all four were hospital cases. They worked quickly, Gail administered the pain-killing gas while Martin dressed the burns as comfortably as he could. Other wounds were dressed and the fractured wrist immobilised. Ted Packer enlisted the help of two tough looking roustabouts to carry the casualties on stretchers to the waiting helicopter.

Martin turned to Gail. 'You go, too. I don't need you here any longer.'

She shook her head. 'If there are any more casualties you will. Can't Mr Packer go with them.'

He frowned. 'It could be dangerous here. I'd rather you left with the patients.'

'I'll take my chance along with you and Kev,' she told him quietly. She turned to the orderly. 'You go with the men, Mr Packer. I'll stay on in case I'm needed and come back with the others on the boat.'

They saw the patients safely on board the helicopter. By now the lifeboat had already made one trip back to shore carrying most of the rig's crew. It was to return for the remaining few, including Martin and Gail. They went back to the mess-room to wait.

Kev appeared a tense half hour later, his face blackened and streaked with sweat. He looked exhausted.

'A set of dodgy valves,' he told them breathlessly, sinking into a chair and gratefully accepting the mug of tea an orderly had brought him. 'It caused severe overheating. Just as well to let things cool down overnight.' He winced as his arm touched the arm of the chair and Gail reached out to him.

'You're hurt!'

As she touched his arm, Kev let out a yell. 'Ouch! That's odd, I never felt it before. Guess I was too busy working against time before that blasted thing exploded again!'

Very carefully, Gail stripped off his overall and shirt sleeve revealing a badly blistered arm.

Martin stepped forward to look. 'You idiot!' he admonished. 'You must have skin like leather not to have noticed this lot!' They worked quickly, but Gail noticed Kev's colour drain as he looked down at the burned arm.

'It's hospital for you with this,' Martin told him. 'At least overnight.'

'Great. Will you bring me some grapes and girlie magazines?' Kev tried to smile but as he looked up at Gail the grin seemed to dissolve.

'Quick! He's going to pass out.' Martin was just in time to catch Kev as he collapsed.

They lowered him to the floor and turned him on to his side. 'He'll be OK,' Martin said. 'A mixture of heat, exhaustion and shock. I'm no engineer, but I do know that whatever he did in that engine room must have been highly dangerous.'

When the lifeboat returned they went on board along with the remaining members of the rig's crew. One by one they were strapped into the inspection cradle and lowered on to the deck. At Martin's insistence Gail went first. She felt very small and vulnerable as she swung precariously over the tossing waves below. But she felt more confident than she would have done, having learned to swim a little on her day at the beach with Kev and Rick. As she swung in the wind above the deck of the small craft tossing below, she knew that if she did fall she would at least have a chance of survival.

All the way back to the shore she cradled Kev's head in her lap while Martin kept a careful check on his pulse and respiration.

Grinning up at Gail as they neared the shore Kev said, 'Maybe this would be a good time to tell Martin we're related!'

'What's that?' Martin raised an enquiring eyebrow at Gail.

'Kev's been tracing his Dorset ancestors,' she explained. 'Going through the church records. He discovered that a woman from his mother's side of the family married a man from yours a couple of hundred years ago.'

Kev grinned at Martin with some of the

old mischief in his eyes. 'How's it feel to have the descendant of a transported convict turning up and claiming kinship?' He winked at Gail and she turned to look at Martin, but he was laughing.

'Nothing I discover about my family can surprise me any more,' he chuckled. '*That* piece of news is definitely on the plus side after what I've seen you do today. When you get out of hospital we'll celebrate it with a bottle of bubbly. In the meantime just try to get some rest, eh?'

At the hospital they saw him settled in the ward and Martin promised to look in on him the following morning.

By the time they came out on to the forecourt it was ten o'clock and a waning moon lit the darkening sky with a soft glow. Gail gave an involuntary sigh.

'Tired?' Martin looked at her.

'A bit. It's been a long day.' She ran a hand through her windswept hair. She must look a sight, but she was too weary to care.

'I hate to remind you, but we've no transport,' Martin said. 'Kev's car is still at Hemmingbury where we left it to pick up the chopper.'

'Of course. I'd forgotten.' She remembered her beautiful and expensive hat, pulled off and tossed uncaringly into the back as they raced for the helicopter.

'I'll collect it for him tomorrow,' Martin

213

said wearily. 'But for now I think it's a taxi for us.'

She must have fallen asleep in the taxi. Coming to as it pulled up, she found her head resting on Martin's shoulder and sat up abruptly.

'Where are we?'

'The surgery.' He paid the driver and helped her out on to the pavement.

'Oh, I – I'd rather go home.' She watched in dismay as the taxi pulled away from the kerb.

He was unlocking the door of the side entrance that led to the flat and he turned to look at her, a frown darkening his face. 'All right. But let me change and clean up first, will you?' As she hesitated on the threshold he said irritably, 'Oh, for God's sake, Gail! If you were brave enough to go out to an oil rig that was threatening to explode, surely ten minutes alone with me can't be so daunting – or *can* it?'

Chastened, she followed him up the stairs, reminded uncomfortably of the evening that she had overheard – and misunderstood – the conversation he was having with Frances.

As he closed the door he looked at her. 'The bathroom's on your left. You can use it. I'll slip downstairs and use the shower in the surgery. You'll find a clean towel in the airing cupboard.'

She shook her head. 'No. It's your flat. You

214

use the bathroom. I can wait till I–'

'Oh, don't argue!' He stopped her words with a glare. 'Have you any idea what you look like?' Taking her arm he bundled her unceremoniously into the bathroom and closed the door behind her.

Immediately she caught sight of herself in a full-length mirror and she winced as she took in her reflection. Her hair, so carefully coiffured for the wedding, now hung about her face in wisps. Her face was streaked with dirt and her beautiful new outfit was crumpled and grubby beyond recognition. Heart sinking, she stripped off her ruined clothes and climbed into the shower, realising as the refreshing warm water caressed her body how bone-weary she was. Who would ever have thought that Celia's wedding day would end like this?

Drying herself on the clean towel she found, Gail put her ruined clothes back on again and combed out her damp hair, regarding her scrubbed face in the mirror as she did so. She had started the day looking her best and ended it looking the worst possible. Ironic! It couldn't matter though, seeing that she would soon be leaving Lullford – and Martin for good.

She found him in the kitchen making coffee. He had changed into jeans and a navy sweat-shirt. His hair was damp, too. It was rumpled where he had been rubbing it with the towel that still hung around his neck. As she came in he turned to look at her.

'Feeling better?'

'A little. My wedding outfit is ruined, though.'

'I dare say you could claim for a new one. Mellex would reimburse you.'

She was shocked. 'I wouldn't dream of it! Maybe if I were to wash it right away I could get the stains out.'

'All right!' He glowered at her. 'I know you hate every minute you're forced to spend with me, but you won't have to endure it much longer. I'll take you home as soon as I've had some coffee.' He turned back to the boiling kettle and busied himself with the coffee. 'If you're worrying about Donaghue, don't. He'll be fine.'

'I know he will, and I wasn't worrying.' She felt her throat thicken. 'Martin – what's wrong?'

He turned, thrusting a mug of coffee into her hands. 'Don't think I can't see how you feel about him, Gail!'

Her eyes widened. 'I told you. He's a friend.'

He shook his head. 'Do you always treat *friends* with such tender loving care? All the way back in the lifeboat – holding his head in your lap – stroking his hair?'

'He was hurt! You said yourself, he'd been

brave! Anyway, what do *you* care?' She was angry now and she took an involuntary step towards him, her eyes bright.

'I shouldn't, should I?' he returned. 'Not after you told me how little you care about me. As a matter of interest, has he asked you to marry him? Are you engaged?'

It took all her control not to stamp her foot with frustration. 'Kev is going home to Australia soon,' she shouted. 'He's going home to ask his childhood sweetheart to marry him. He asked my advice about it. *That's* the kind of relationship we have, Martin.'

'I see! How *cosy*. So you weep on each other's shoulders, do you? I suppose you've discussed me with him, too!'

'I told him I'd given my notice,' she said between clenched teeth, 'and that we'd quarrelled. And if you really want to know, he advised me to try to put things right between us.'

Martin turned away. 'Oh? That was big of him!'

'He said second chances don't always come along.'

As he turned towards her again she saw that the anger had dissolved from his face. For a long moment they stood looking at each other. Finally Gail drew a sigh and turned towards the door.

'I'd better go.'

At once his hand shot out to grasp her shoulder. '*Don't* – don't go.' He ran a hand through his damp, rumpled hair and threw the towel on to the worktop. 'Oh, Gail. I'm sorry, darling.'

She raised tear-filled eyes to his face. 'So am I. Oh, why is it always like this, Martin?'

'It needn't be. *It won't be.*' Roughly, he pulled her into his arms and held her close. 'You were marvellous out there on the rig. I was so proud of you. Kev, too. He's a good bloke, I know that. But seeing you with him like that, so comfortable; so *at ease;* the way you and I have never been–'

'We haven't had a chance, Martin,' she said. 'Ever since I came here everything seems to have been against our getting to know each other better.'

'It can change,' he said quietly, his lips against her ear. 'It *will* change. If you want it to – if it isn't too late, that is.'

She looked up at him. 'Oh, Martin, it isn't too late. I didn't mean the things I said. I *do* want it to change. If you only knew how much. If only I'd known what was happening.'

'I'd made up my mind to tell you everything that night at the flat,' he told her. 'But you didn't come, so I assumed I'd left it too late and you'd given up on me.' He sighed. 'Don't you see, darling, it was having nothing to offer you except debts and problems that stopped me from telling you. I felt it wasn't fair to involve you. I wanted to get it all sorted out first.'

'But I *was* involved, Martin,' she told him. 'I've been involved from the beginning; from the moment I first set eyes on you. Didn't you know that?'

'I hoped. That's why I wanted to have you near me – to work with me. Then suddenly I was plunged into the mess my father left. It seemed I was destined to make everyone miserable in some way or the other. It didn't seem fair to drag you into it with me. When you said you were leaving, that you didn't care any more, I tried – I really *tried* – to feel glad.'

She slipped her arms around his waist and held him close. 'Oh, Martin, you idiot! If you only knew how unhappy I've been. When I thought that you and Frances...' She sighed. 'There's an awful lot about me you have to learn.'

'I realised that this evening – seeing you with Kev. It struck me forcibly that he knew you better than I ever have.' He looked down at her. 'And it hurt, Gail – it hurt like hell. I've never felt so damned jealous in my life!'

When his lips claimed hers she responded with all the love she'd tried to deny for so long, clinging to him desperately as though she would never let him go.

'I love you,' he told her over and over between kisses. His hand cupped her face and his eyes looked into hers. 'When I saw you at the church this afternoon I thought you looked more beautiful than I'd ever seen you. But now – like this with your hair damp and your face scrubbed and shiny you're lovely – know that?' His voice was soft and husky, 'Warm and soft and lovely.' He drew her close. 'Say you'll stay, Gail – that you love me too – that you'll marry me?' His eyes searched hers and suddenly a laugh of sheer joy bubbled up inside her.

'I love you – and of course I'll stay,' she told him, her voice catching. 'I'd just like to see anyone try and stop me, Dr Hannerford! I'd like–'

But Martin didn't wait to hear the rest of her sentence. This was no time for talking, as he told her later. There would be plenty of time for that. Just now there were more urgent priorities.

The publishers hope that this book has given you enjoyable reading. Large Print Books are especially designed to be as easy to see and hold as possible. If you wish a complete list of our books please ask at your local library or write directly to:

Dales Large Print Books
Magna House, Long Preston,
Skipton, North Yorkshire.
BD23 4ND

This Large Print Book, for people
who cannot read normal print,
is published under the auspices of

THE ULVERSCROFT FOUNDATION

J.P.